The Witch's Candelabra

J.B. Lesel

Copyright 2020 J.B. Lesel

Copyright © 2023 J.B. Lesel All rights reserved.

The characters and events portrayed in this book are fictitious. Any similarity to real persons, living or dead, is coincidental and not intended by the author.

No part of this book may be reproduced, or stored in a retrieval system, or transmitted in any form or by any means, electronic, mechanical, photocopying, recording, or otherwise, without express written permission of the publisher.

Table of Contents

Chapter 1 - Ghosts of Shared Fears 6

Chapter 2 - The Pawn Shop's Enchantment 18

Chapter 3- The Candelabra's Dance 24

Chapter 4 - The Enigmatic Visitor 36

Chapter 5 - Veil of Shadows 52

Chapter 6 - Marketplace Enigma 59

Chapter 7 - Beneath the Surface 74

Chapter 8 - Invisible Echoes of Enchantment 90

Chapter 9 - Ethereal Currents and Unseen Threads 109

Chapter 10 - Melodies 124

Chapter 11 - Levitation 133

Chapter 12 - Shadows and Whispers 136

Chapter 13 - Mysteries Unraveled 143

Chapter 14 - Enigmatic Alliances 152

Chapter 15 - Cautious Engagements 160

Chapter 16 - Echoes of Dreams 164

Chapter 17 - Unveiled Secrets 168

Chapter 18 - Clashing Perspectives 174

Chapter 19 - Ethereal Reflections 178

Chapter 20 - The Chase Intensifies 186

Chapter 21 - Threshold of Revelations 201

Chapter 22 - Altered Paths 208

Chapter 23 - Rediscovery in Silence 221

Chapter 24 - The Spellbound House 225

Chapter 25 - A Confrontation's Edge 235

Chapter 26 - Awakening of Purpose 247

Chapter 27 - Ethereal Bonds 260

Chapter 1 - Ghosts of Shared Fears

Braids:

The boys pursued the dusky dog, ruffling its fur with sticks as they sped past on swift bikes. Their wheels ground and slid, alternating between the pebbled path and the grass beside it. Seated on a picnic blanket, I observed the scene: boys tormenting the poor creature. People truly do suck. Perhaps they ought to experience a taste of their own medicine. Delving into my pocket, I retrieved some magic dust—or rather, cinnamon. Plucking a leaf from the nearby oak tree, I crushed it finely into the cinnamon with a lit alight hand.

The tree, with its sinewy whip-like branches, curled and extended. One thick branch reached out, entangling itself in the bike wheel of one of the circling boys. This caused his tires to skid to a halt, catapulting him onto the ground. His companions, caught in a domino effect, crashed their bikes amidst trampling and shouting. Their entangled bikes twisted into scraps of metal as their bodies were hurled through the air. Amidst this chaos, the dog seized its chance to escape. I beckoned it over with a wave of dried meat, which it gratefully devoured, slobbering my hands with sticky, warm saliva. I tenderly stroked its head with my free hand, and it responded with a happy wag of its tail.

The tree was not yet finished. It wrapped a branch around the ankles of two boys, hoisting them into the air. They were plugged into a hole of its gnarled trunk, their bottoms slapped by wiry sapling branches.

My picnic concluded, I closed my book and traversed the damp grass, its fresh scent filling the air, towards the street beyond.

Here, the houses stood decorated and ancient, a testament to times long past. Men donned suits while women sported frills and wonderful hats. Yet beneath this beautiful attire, the people were hollow. They wandered through their lives devoid of passion. It seemed as if not a single soul in town harbored an imaginative thought. Their outlook on life was disheartening; devoid of aspirations or fanciful dreams. Should anyone dare to harbor such a desire or passion, it would likely go unrecognized in this lackluster world.

I made my way to the local pub, a place where I was a familiar face. Turning a corner, I stepped inside. It was still late afternoon, far too early for the happy hour crowd of non-regulars.

***

The room was as dreary as ever, filled with the same sad regulars. But who was I to judge? I walked up to the bar, where the bartender, a man with a ginger mustache, turned to greet me. Just for the record, I'm of legal drinking age.

"Steam engine," I requested, a concoction of unsavory saffron rose.

"Right away, Miss Braids," he replied with a nod.

As I waited, a man's shout cut through the room. "Hey you, pretty love!" He moved closer to me, his intentions clear. I reached deep into my pocket, feeling for the soft dust between my fingers. With a swift motion, a puff of blue, thick smoke burst in his face. When it cleared, he had transformed – a grotesque pig-nosed monster.

"What the!??" he started, staggering back in shock and anger.

That'll show him.

I took a swig from my shot glass and tossed some coins to the bartender. Suddenly, a surge of greenness coursed through my body. I needed to leave... fast. Staggering into the bathroom, clutching my chest, I tried to lock the door, but it burst open. The pig-nosed man was right in my face.

"Hey, missy, you aren't getting away so easy. I don't care what I look like..." He tried to wrestle me against the wall, but as he held my wrists, they began to fade, turning transparent and ghostly. I couldn't help but give him a smug look, the nausea fading from my face.

A sizzling sound filled the air, and smoke burst forth from where our skin made contact. Green flames on my hand ignited into a larger blue flame, casting the room in shadowy blue light. I could still see the other people in the room, but they appeared dark, faint, and wobbly.

Easily pulling away like a ghost, I slammed him with a spell. He crashed, shocked and confused, unconscious on the floor or maybe right into the toilet. The room spun around him... until it seemed upside down. No, I was the one on the ceiling, my complexion a transparent green.

I glided out of the bathroom and into the bar room, where all the regular patrons were now on the ceiling. The upside-down room was dark and dreary, filled with brown crossbeams. Blue, shadowy figures sat upon these beams – demons, perhaps? But I wasn't afraid. Stepping forward on the ceiling, I approached the figures, clearing a spider web off a dusty old crossbeam before taking a seat.

I floated into the rafters, where ghosts glowed dimly. They played poker, sitting on the wooden beams, using a ghost table or chandelier as their table.

As I floated closer, the ghosts turned to look at me. There was a drawn-out, eerie silence, thick with suspense. I could feel their ghostly eyes, or in some cases, the empty sockets where eyes should have been, fixating on me. "Boys, deal me in," I said, my voice echoing slightly in the spectral air.

They continued to stare, their appearances grotesque and ghastly. Their pale, blue forms shimmered faintly in the dim light. One ghost, his head missing, seemed to gaze at me with an invisible stare. Another, lacking a shoe, floated slightly lopsided, his foot a mere wisp of mist.

After a moment that stretched like eternity, one of them spoke. His voice was like the rustling of dry leaves, a whisper from beyond. "You're brave to join us, Miss Braids," he said, the gap where his head should have been somehow not hindering his speech. "But are you ready to play with the likes of us?"

I couldn't help but smile, a chill of excitement running down my spine. This was exactly the kind of distraction I needed. "I've played with worse," I replied confidently, taking my seat on a crossbeam beside them. "What's the game?"

The black-haired ghost chuckled, a sound like wind whistling through a hollow cavern. "It's a game of fate and chance, much like life itself. But be warned, the stakes are higher when you're playing with the departed."

I nodded, ready for whatever challenge lay ahead. As the cards were dealt, the ghostly figures around me seemed to grow more solid, their ethereal forms gaining substance in the flickering blue light. I was about to engage in a game that was more than just cards and wagers; it was a dance with the echoes of the past, a flirtation with the unknown.

As the game progressed, the atmosphere thickened with unspoken words and glances that lingered a second too long. I felt a strange kinship with these spectral beings, yet a gulf of unbridgeable experiences separated us.

"You know, I've always been afraid of people," I confessed, my voice barely more than a whisper. "Afraid to act, to face the darkness within and around me." My fingers fiddled with the cards, a nervous habit I couldn't shake.

The ghosts nodded, their movements slow and deliberate. "We lived like that in life," murmured the ghost with the missing shoe, his voice tinged with regret. "Always in fear, never daring to change our fate."

I sighed, a sense of camaraderie building in the gloom. "That's exactly why I find solace in your company. You're the closest to understanding me. People... they just suck. They're too caught up in their own lives to see what's really happening around them."

The black-haired ghost chimed in, his voice echoing as if from a distant place. "That's true. In life, we were too cowardly to make a difference, too scared to step out of our comfort zones. Now, in death, we're just echoes of those fears, unable to change the world or ourselves."

I leaned back, absorbing their words. It was a bittersweet realization that these ghosts, stuck in their eternal limbo, were my closest confidants. They couldn't affect the living world, and they never did in their own lifetimes. In a way, they were as powerless as I felt among the living.

"This is why I can only trust and confide in you," I said to the group, a hint of melancholy in my voice. "You understand the paralysis of fear, the inability to act. You're as close to understanding me as anyone ever could."

They looked at me, compassion in their eyes, and the game continued, but my thoughts wandered. I was amongst friends who were bound by their past fears, just as I was constrained by my own. In this dim, upside-down world, amidst these spectral figures, I found an odd sense of belonging. Yet, it was also a stark reminder of the isolating power of fear and the comfort of shared understanding in the unlikeliest of places.

Chapter 2 - The Pawn Shop's Enchantment

Braids:

I perched behind the ancient, scarred desk in my father's pawn shop, my fingers drumming an uneven rhythm on the worn wood. Each tap echoed softly in the cluttered, shadow-draped room, filled with whispers of forgotten histories. This week, keeping to myself was a necessary task amidst the cluttered confines of the shop.

The pawn shop was a labyrinth of forgotten stories, each item whispering its history: the tarnished brass telescope that seemed to still hold stardust, the velvet-lined jewelry box that hummed a long-lost lullaby, and the rusted swords that echoed distant battle cries. But ever since I was a little girl, I had found wonder in this ever-changing collection of potential treasures. The assortment of gadgets never ceased to intrigue me, though the charisma required to sell them was a different story entirely.

A customer, clad in a blue suit that hung a bit too loose on his frame, meandered down the main aisle. His eyes, bright with a child-like curiosity, darted from one relic to another, each piece telling its own silent, mysterious story. As I passed by, he looked up with an inquisitive expression. "What's this for?" he asked, clearly intrigued.

I paused, my gaze lingering on him with a thinly veiled mix of disdain and curiosity. In the dim light of the shop, my shadowed eyes might have seemed just a touch too cold, too distant. "It crushes nuts," I replied flatly. "Walnuts, in particular." I eyed his face again, noting his transition from startled to oddly joyous.

He eagerly announced his intention to buy the contraption. Following me to the counter, he watched as I rang up the sale on the old cash register. "Ten pounds," I stated, maintaining an expression of glassy-eyed indifference, my fancy black outfit adding to my aloof demeanor.

As the customer left, the bell above the door jingling in his wake, I didn't spare a thought for the irony of the transaction. In this pawn shop, amidst the clutter of discarded dreams and secondhand memories, transactions were just a part of the routine — another oddity in a place brimming with them. It was my normal, a world away from the ceilings of ghost-filled bars and the comfort of familiar spirits. Here, in the dusty reality of the pawn shop, I found a different kind of solace, one rooted in the mundane and the unremarkable.

"If you'll excuse me, my shift is over," I announced, already making my way to the creaking wooden staircase. The steps groaned under my feet, a familiar chorus to my daily routine. Reaching the top, I called out, "Dad, your shift is ready."

In the kitchen, I found my father, Jean-Louis, engrossed in one of his cherished activities. He was hunched over a thick, leather-bound book, its pages yellowed with age. His passion for ancient texts and obscure historical accounts was evident in the way his eyes danced over the words, a look of pure contentment on his face.

"Braids?" Aunt Biddi's voice cut through the tranquility. I turned to see her lumbering over, her figure round and motherly in a way that only Aunt Biddi could be. From my perspective, she had always been larger than life, both in stature and in presence.

As a child, Aunt Biddi was my mentor and my warden. She kept me under her watchful eye, a strictness in her demeanor that rarely allowed for childish play. My father, occupied with the pawn shop and somewhat meek in Aunt Biddi's commanding presence, never interfered. She was always vocal about her beliefs on child-rearing, despite never having children of her own. Her opinions, strong and unwavering, shaped much of my early life.

I glanced at my father, who seemed too absorbed in his book to notice the exchange. Seizing the opportunity, I muttered a quick incantation under my breath — a little spell to slip away unnoticed. The words were soft, barely a whisper, but their effect was immediate. A shroud of unnoticeability enveloped me, allowing me to move past Aunt Biddi without drawing her attention.

Under the guise of adjusting my sleeve, I subtly weaved a spell, fingers tracing arcane symbols unseen by anyone. A faint shimmer of magic, invisible to the untrained eye, cloaked me in a veil of inconspicuousness. As I slipped away, unnoticed by the watchful eyes of my aunt and father, a twinge of guilt tugged at my conscience, mingling with the thrill of my clandestine escape.

Aunt Biddi, a towering figure in both stature and spirit, had always loomed large in my life. Her presence was like a constant, heavy cloud - dark and foreboding, yet undeniably necessary for the rain that nourishes the earth. For all her overbearing ways, a sternness that often felt like an unyielding storm, there was an undercurrent of duty and love as relentless and deep as the ocean. Her eyes, sharp as hawk's, missed nothing and softened for nothing, yet in their depths, if one looked hard enough, there flickered a flame of fierce protection and unwavering commitment.

She had wrapped me in her world of strict routines and rigid expectations, a world where every action was a lesson, and every word a teaching. I remembered the countless evenings spent under her watchful eye, her voice a steady cadence as she imparted wisdom about the ancient arts, the secrets of our lineage, and the weight of our legacy. Each word was spoken with a reverence for our heritage and a solemn hope for my future.

In her own, unspoken way, Aunt Biddi had been my anchor in the tumultuous seas of adolescence. Her brand of love was not warm, nor was it gentle, but it was as solid and real as the ground beneath our feet. It was a love born from duty, yes, but also from a deep-seated belief in the importance of strength, resilience, and the unwavering courage to face the shadows of the world.

Though I often chafed under her strict guidance, feeling the cold shadow of her expectations looming over me, I couldn't deny the foundation she had built within me. In her insistence on discipline and control, she had unwittingly taught me the value of independence and the power of my own will. And for that, despite the many storms we weathered together, a part of me was profoundly grateful."

But in that moment, what I yearned for was a breath of solitude, a fleeting escape from Aunt Biddi's ever-present gaze. As I slipped into my room, the door closing with a soft click behind me, I exhaled a sigh that felt like it had been building all day, heavy with the unspoken thoughts and unexpressed frustrations. The sound echoed slightly in the stillness, mingling with the faint, whisper-like rustle of my drapes stirred by a gentle night breeze.

My gaze drifted slowly over the room, taking in the eclectic array of objects arrayed on the shelves and walls – each a fragment of my own, deeply personal universe. Here, a crystalline vial filled with a swirling, luminescent concoction I had brewed under a new moon. There, an ancient book with pages so delicate I feared they might crumble to dust under too harsh a touch, its cryptic text a language only my eyes could unravel. Every item, a piece of my hidden self, stood in stark, almost rebellious contrast to the orderly, mundane clutter of the pawn shop below.

This room was my haven, a sanctuary where the walls themselves seemed to understand the need for silence and secrecy. Here, I could let the mask of indifference slip, allowing my true self to surface in the privacy of my own space. Surrounded by the quiet comfort of my collected oddities, each with its own story and significance, I felt a sense of peace and belonging that eluded me in the outside world.

I moved through the room, my fingers tracing over the objects with a tenderness I seldom showed. To an outsider, these items might seem mere curios, but to me, they were talismans, each holding a memory, a secret, a piece of my soul. In their silent company, I could let my thoughts unfurl, untangled from the expectations and demands of the world outside these four walls. Here, in the dim, soft light of my sanctuary, I was truly free – free to dream, to remember, to be unapologetically myself.

I lingered among my treasures a moment longer, allowing their silent stories to wash over me. Yet, as the moon rose higher, casting elongated shadows across my room, a sense of restlessness began to stir within me. It was as if the night itself whispered of mysteries yet to be unraveled, calling me to explore the hidden corners of my own world.

With a reluctant glance at my collection, I felt the pull of the nocturnal world beyond these walls. The need to wander, to immerse myself in the quiet solace of the night was irresistible. There was something enchanting about the house when shrouded in darkness, a different kind of magic that beckoned me.

I rose, my movements slow and deliberate, as if breaking a spell that bound me to this sanctuary. My hand brushed against the cold, iron skeleton key in my pocket, its intricate design a familiar comfort. It was time to venture out, to lose myself in the moonlit corridors of the house and the secret garden that awaited under the watchful eye of the stars.

As I stepped towards the door, a sense of anticipation mingled with an indefinable apprehension. The night held secrets, and I, a willing seeker, was about to uncover them. Each creak of the stairs under my feet seemed to echo louder in the stillness, a rhythmic accompaniment to the pounding of my heart. Little did I know, as I ascended towards the mysteries of the night, that something unexpected awaited me, a small, yet significant alteration in the familiar landscape of my nocturnal wanderings.

Chapter 3- The Candelabra's Dance

Braids:

As I ascended the narrow staircase, each step groaned underfoot, their creaks resounding in the quiet house. Reaching the top, a sudden obstacle nearly tripped me – a neatly folded dark square on the wooden floor. Recognizing the fresh linens, a quiet offering from Aunt Biddy, I paused. Her attempts at care were often cloaked in silent gestures like these, though she never crossed the threshold into my personal domain. My room, after all, was my sanctuary, guarded not just by the physical lock but by the unspoken rules we both silently acknowledged.

Fishing out the iron skeleton key from the deep pocket of my skirt, I admired its ornate, cold metalwork for a moment. This key, with its intricate design and familiar chill against my skin, was more than just a tool; it was a symbol of the private world I kept. Gently, I inserted it into the lock, feeling the tumblers yield as it turned with a satisfying clank. The bolts slid back, granting me access to my inner sanctum once more

Once inside, I surveyed the draping that hung from the ceiling. With a casual swish of my hand, the fabric crinkled and retracted, neatly tucking itself into the room's edges. This small act of magic framed the ceiling windows perfectly, allowing the silvery moonlight to cast an ethereal glow into the room. I lit the kerosene lamps, their gentle light soothing to the eye, and took a deep breath, savoring the calm ambiance.

Through the window, my rooftop garden was visible. It was a small, enchanting space, filled with a variety of herbs and flowers that thrived under the moon's watchful eye. The garden was my sanctuary, a place where nature and magic intertwined seamlessly.

The room itself was sparsely furnished, with a simple bed tucked in one corner and my work desk dominating the other. I placed the folded linens on my bed, adding to the current disarray of sheets. My desk, a large assembly of mismatched wooden tables scavenged from the street over the years, was a testament to my eclectic tastes. It was cluttered with bowls of mortar and pestle, their surfaces stained with the remnants of various spices.

In the heart of this organized chaos sat a large, glistening silver candelabra. Intricately carved with four flame holders, it was the centerpiece of my magical practice. Beside it, propped on a tilted oaken stand, lay my spell book. Its pages were filled with my handwriting, a collection of scribbles, spells, and notes accumulated over time. Around the book, rows of glass jars lined the desk, each containing spices of all colors and kinds. Cinnamon sticks, dried lavender, and crushed rose petals were just a few of the ingredients that filled the jars, their scents mingling in the air, creating an atmosphere ripe for magic and creativity.

This room, with its blend of the mundane and the mystical, was a reflection of who I was — a haven where I could be my true self, unfettered by the expectations and norms of the outside world.

Before I could even take a step towards my table, a sudden movement at the corner of my eye startled me. I spun around, heart racing, as a flurry of black birds crashed against the window, their caws loud and demanding. "Okay, okay!" I cried out, hurrying to open the window.

The birds, a raucous group of crows, surged into the room as soon as the window was ajar. They swooped and dived, filling the air with a cacophony of trills and flaps. I watched as they perched on every available surface of my room - the bookshelves, the back of my chair, even atop the candelabra, their beady eyes watching me expectantly.

I dashed to my supply of birdseed, kept for moments just like this. Grabbing handfuls of the seed, I threw it out the window onto the deck of my garden. Normally, I would meticulously place the seeds in the designated feeders, taking care to spread them evenly. But today, my patience was thin; I wasn't in the mood for such intricacies.

The crows cackled and took off in a frenzy, diving towards the scattered seed. Their black wings beat against the moonlit sky, creating a whirlwind of feathers and energy. I watched them for a moment, their wildness a stark contrast to the calmness of my room. Once they were all outside, I closed the window, the silence settling in once more.

Sighing, I brushed off my hands and turned back to my desk. The crows, with their unexpected visit, had disrupted my train of thought, but their departure left a renewed sense of tranquility. I smiled to myself, thinking how even in this small space, high above the streets, nature found a way to remind me of the world outside.

Approaching my table, I began the delicate task of mixing the spices, each one selected for its specific magical properties. The air was soon filled with a medley of aromas — earthy, sweet, and pungent. I carefully measured and ground the ingredients, my hands moving with practiced ease.

Once the mixture was ready, I turned my attention to the candelabra. Its silver surface gleamed in the lamplight, waiting to play its part in the spellwork. I carefully placed a portion of the spice mixture into each of the candelabra's four holders, my fingers deftly maneuvering the delicate ingredients.

Lighting the candelabra, I watched as the flames caught hold of the spices, sending curls of scented smoke into the air. This was more than just a ritual of burning; it was the alchemy of transformation. As the spices burned, their essence was released, mingling with the magic inherent in the flames. This process was crucial for creating spell materials –

each ingredient contributing its unique energy to the spell I would later cast.

The flames danced and flickered, casting a warm, enchanting glow across the room. I watched, entranced, as the ingredients transformed, their physical forms consumed by fire, leaving behind only their magical essence. This essence would be captured and stored within the candelabra, ready to be harnessed when the time was right.

This dynamic of spell logic, where the physical becomes the magical through the act of burning, was a fundamental aspect of my craft. It was a process of conversion, of taking something ordinary and imbuing it with extraordinary power. In the world of magic, the boundaries between the mundane and the mystical were often blurred, and it was in this liminal space that my power thrived.

As the last of the spices turned to ash and the flames died down, I felt a sense of accomplishment. The candelabra now held within it the potential for powerful spells, the energy of the burnt spices lying dormant until called upon. I closed my spellbook, content with the night's work, and prepared to settle in for the evening, the room still filled with the lingering scent of magic and mystery.

Reflecting on the night's work, I was suddenly transported back in time to a defining moment from my childhood. It was the first time I had ever attempted to use the candelabra, a time when I was still naive to the ways of magic and its unpredictable nature.

Back then, I had sneaked into my room, the candelabra held tightly in my young hands, my heart pounding with a mix of excitement and fear. I had locked the door, keenly aware of Aunt Biddi's disapproval of anything remotely magical. She had always viewed magic with suspicion, and I knew my secret experiments would not sit well with her.

With a sense of urgency, I had set up the candelabra, the room around me quiet except for the occasional creak of the house. I remember placing the spices into the holders, my hands shaking slightly with anticipation. Lighting the candelabra, I expected nothing more than a small, controlled flame.

However, what happened next was beyond my wildest expectations. The flames erupted with a life of their own, dancing and swirling in a frenzied display. I stood there, frozen in shock and awe, as the room filled with a thick, fragrant smoke. The candelabra, it seemed, had a mind of its own.

Suddenly, Aunt Biddi's voice shattered the moment. "Braids! What are you doing in there?" she demanded, her knocks on the door echoing through the room. In my panic, I didn't know what to do. I had no spells or incantations to call upon, no knowledge of how to control the wild magic that I had unleashed.

But then, as if sensing my desperation, the candelabra reacted. The smoke, instead of choking the room, began to move in mysterious patterns. It twirled and spun, forming shapes and figures that danced around the room in a mesmerizing display. It was as if the candelabra was protecting me, creating a magical spectacle to keep Aunt Biddi at bay.

The smoke swirled into images of mythical creatures and enchanted forests, a beautiful chaos that held me spellbound.

The banging on the door faded into the background, muffled by the magic that filled the room.

As the last wisps of smoke vanished, leaving behind a lingering scent of burnt spices, I realized the candelabra was more than just an object; it was a gateway to a world of magic I had yet to understand. That moment marked the beginning of my journey into the mystical, a journey filled with awe, wonder, and the respect for the untamed power that lay within the candelabra.

This memory, vivid and alive, brought a smile to my face as I stood in my room, years later, now a seasoned practitioner of magic. The candelabra, once a source of unexpected chaos, had become an integral part of my life, a symbol of the magical path I had chosen.

Chapter 4 - The Enigmatic Visitor

Braids:

That afternoon, years ago, I found myself playing in a corner of my father's pawn shop. I was dressing up a mannequin twice my size, having adorned it with a large black hat and some sequined clothing. The shop, with its myriad of curiosities, was my playground.

It was a period of upheaval for us. My mother had just left, leaving me and my dad to our own devices. Aunt Biddy hadn't yet moved in with her overbearing ways. How little did we know that her arrival would change everything.

"Excuse me, is anyone here?" A woman's voice disrupted my play. She stood at the counter, a vision in pink, her dress and feathered sunhat starkly contrasting with the shop's dusty ambiance. The potent aroma of her rose perfume filled the air. It was a quiet day, devoid of other customers.

My father, a middle-aged man with a kind face, emerged from the back room at the sound of the bell. "How can I help you, ma'am?" he asked, his voice gentle and accommodating.

The woman, with an air of impatience, slammed a heavy box onto the counter. "I need to get rid of this junk. This is a junk store, isn't it?" she snapped.

"We buy goods of value, if that's what you wish," my dad began, but she cut him off.

"I don't want any money for this junk. My husband's mother passed away, and he wouldn't let me throw it away. Do I look like I need the pennies this might be worth? I don't need the money, or the memories..." She sneered at the box as if it offended her.

My dad, ever the peacemaker, offered, "Would you like a donation receipt, then?"

"A what?" she scoffed.

"It's just to prove you gave it to a pawn shop and didn't just toss it away," he explained.

She waved her hand dismissively, her gold bracelets jingling. "Fine, just give me the receipt. I have better places to be." She tapped her red heels impatiently as my dad wrote up the receipt.

"Here you are, madam. One donation receipt for 'one box of goods,'" he said, handing it to her. She snatched it with her elegantly manicured fingers and strutted out. I watched her from behind the mannequin, her heels echoing on the cobblestone street long after she disappeared from sight.

"What a strange lady," my dad remarked, lifting me onto the counter.

"And in quite the hurry!" Aunt Biddy chimed in, emerging from the back room with her usual plump cheeriness.

Little did we know then, the contents of that box would introduce me to a world beyond my wildest imagination. The candelabra that lay within would become the cornerstone of my journey into magic.

***

"Yes, Papa! What kind of treasures did she leave for us?" I asked with childlike excitement.

My father, Jean-Louis, peered into the box, which seemed filled with miscellaneous household objects beneath white doilies. He began laying them out on the counter, and I leaned in eagerly over his shoulder. Beneath the doilies were some tea cups, a pot, and then, an old silver candelabra with five cups, lying horizontally. With his notebook beside him, he cataloged each item meticulously.

"Alright, calm down, Adelia!" he said, lifting me onto the side of the counter where my legs dangled freely, keeping me a safe distance from the box. "No touching yet, I need to catalog everything first!"

Despite his warning, I couldn't help but be drawn to the contents of the box. My gaze fixed on the silver candelabra. It sparkled as the light from outside illuminated its engraved floral etchings. Despite the caked red wax in its holders, remnants of long-ago burnings, it had such character. The wax dripped off the silver branches like frozen waterfalls of blood.

"This is where the little demons dance..." I whispered, utterly captivated by its beauty. My imagination ran wild with the various oddities that came into our shop. Unlike most girls my age, I was fascinated by the uncanny, such as an old doll, scratched and missing an eye. The peculiar and eerie gave me a thrill, and this candelabra was a perfect addition to my collection.

"Some of these need polishing, but they're all of good quality and condition," my father remarked, half to himself, half to me.

"Oh, Father, can I please have this one?" I asked, gripping the candelabra tightly with both hands. "How can I say no to that face?" he sighed. I was a good girl, always helping out in the store, and he often let me pick something from our inventory as a treat.

"But Adelia, this candelabra might be the most valuable thing here. If it's real silver, it could be worth quite a bit. How about I find you another one to play with?"

I pondered this for a moment. I was a practical child but also deeply sentimental. "But Papa, if you let me keep it, its value will increase in the future because it will have been loved and cherished by someone!"

My father laughed. "I don't know about that, but I suppose it's true enough. You can hold onto it until you grow bored of it, as long as you take good care of it."

"Wonderful!" I exclaimed, clapping my hands together. "But just so you know, I'll cherish it forever. You can sell it after that, I suppose, if you're not a skeleton by then."

My father chuckled, agreeing to my terms.

Aunt Biddi, busy arranging doilies on a shelf, chimed in. "I'm sure she'll grow bored of it eventually. Once she does, we can sell it at a good price. Silver retains its value."

"It's almost time for your lessons, Adelia," she reminded me.

"Yes, Aunt Biddi," I replied, my mind still lingering on the candelabra and the adventures we would have together.

***

Clutching the candelabra, I made my way to my room. Our family's flat, situated above the pawn shop, was a world of its own. My room, though small, was my personal haven, a cozy space filled with odds and ends from the shop below.

In this room, amidst my treasures and trinkets, I felt a sense of belonging. I didn't have any friends, no other children to share my peculiar world with. Being homeschooled by Aunt Biddi, I was cut off from the usual avenues of childhood friendships. My shyness didn't help either. The neighborhood kids, who played in the streets and alleys, seemed like creatures from another world. I watched them sometimes from my window, but the thought of approaching them filled me with an inexplicable anxiety.

So, I created my own companions in my room. Each object from the shop had its own story, its own personality. I would spend hours talking to them, weaving elaborate tales and adventures. The candelabra, now a part of this eclectic family, was set on my small wooden desk. I admired its intricate design, the way it caught the light and threw it across the walls, creating patterns that danced and flickered.

I imagined the candelabra had seen grand parties and intimate gatherings, its flames illuminating conversations and secrets. It was not just an object to me; it was a gateway to a world of stories and histories, a silent witness to moments long passed.

In this room, with my imaginary friends and the newly acquired candelabra, I was content. I didn't feel the absence of human companionship as acutely. Here, I was the mistress of my own universe, a place where my shyness couldn't reach me, and where my imagination was free to roam wild and unbound.

After my lesson with Aunt Biddi, a burst of creativity overtook me. I knew exactly what I wanted to do — it was time for a bit of unconventional dress-up, not for myself, but for the candelabra. I rummaged through the house, gathering a variety of items: some tinsel to drape over its silver arms, a bit of cooking oil from the kitchen, and a string from Auntie's sewing kit. I was determined to see how these items would interact with the flames.

Feeling like a true alchemist, I also swiped a few sheets of parchment and a box of matches from my father's cupboard. Once back in my room, I carefully arranged my gathered items around the candelabra, my heart racing with excitement.

First, I drizzled the cooking oil over the parchment, watching as it soaked up the liquid. Then, with a matchstick in hand, I set the parchment alight. It caught fire instantly, burning with a mesmerizing flame that transformed the paper into delicate ashes. The way the parchment curled and disintegrated was almost magical, captivating me entirely.

Emboldened by this initial success, my curiosity about burning other things grew. What would happen if I tried different materials? What colors would they produce, and how would the flames react? The candelabra, once a mere object of beauty, had now become an instrument of discovery in my hands.

I experimented with various items, each burn revealing new wonders and secrets. The tinsel, when lit, created a shower of sparkling embers, while the string from Auntie's sewing kit burned with a slow, steady flame. Each new material added to the candelabra's charm, transforming it from a simple household item into a source of endless fascination and mystery.

In those moments, alone with my candelabra and my experiments, I felt a surge of joy and freedom. The world outside, with its expectations and rules, faded away. Here, in the confines of my room, I was a scientist, an artist, and a magician, all rolled into one. The candelabra, my willing accomplice, stood as a testament to the boundless possibilities that lay within the simplest of things.

***

One day, I found myself standing behind the worn wooden desk of my father's pawn shop, the gloomy interior lending an air of dark mystique to the place. Boredom was a constant companion, as I tried desperately to maintain a facade of professionalism, just in case a customer—or rather, her father—were to wander in. My gaze drifted down, and I idly picked at my black-painted fingernails, a reflection of my dark and enigmatic nature. Unbeknownst to the world, a pair of glorious dusky wings graced my back, a secret I held close to my heart.

The bell above the door, ancient and weathered, suddenly came to life with a melodious chime, announcing the arrival of a visitor. My eyes, still lost in the abyss of my thoughts, slowly lifted as I continued to caress my fingers, painted like midnight itself. The newcomer, a tall, slender man adorned in a fetching suit and top hat, approached the desk with measured grace. His narrow face was etched with a serene yet enigmatic expression, and his deep, concerned brown eyes held a wisdom that hinted at secrets lurking beneath. His thin, elegant nose seemed to cut through the dim light, adding an air of refinement to his enigmatic presence. This was a man who warranted my attention, a departure from the usual casual browsers who frequented our establishment.

"Excuse me, madam," he began with polite eloquence, his words like a siren's call, beckoning me to a deeper mystery. How could I resist such intrigue?

I remained poised, my own demeanor matching the ethereal ambiance of the shop. "Yes, sir," I replied, my voice low and dripping with intrigue. "I have a request, I'm looking for a very specific object, perhaps you have seen it here. It's an old candelabra with five wicks, crafted from silver and metal, about yea high." He raised his hand, motioning a distance of roughly a foot and a half.

My heart threatened to burst from my chest as I gazed into those intense, soulful eyes. It couldn't be... How had he stumbled upon the key to my clandestine world?

Chapter 5 - Veil of Shadows

Braids:

As the last echoes of the man's footsteps faded, the pawn shop returned to its usual stillness, a stillness that hung heavily around me like a thick, invisible cloak. I stood there for a moment, lost in thought, the silence amplifying the turmoil within. It was strange how the ordinary and the extraordinary often intertwined in my life, how the mundane reality of the shop could so suddenly be pierced by the needle of the unexpected.

I brushed my hands over my black apron, a futile attempt to wipe away the residue of anxiety that clung to me. The bell's chime still resonated in my mind, a harbinger of change, or perhaps a test of my resolve. The shop, with its myriad of memories and secrets, felt smaller somehow, as if the walls were inching closer, privy to the storm brewing inside me. It was here, in this sanctuary of the lost and found, that I had learned to hide in plain sight, to blend my truth with the lies required for survival.

I kept my expression inscrutable, my features hidden behind a calm facade. He would never discover the truth about me. I played the part of the concerned pawnshop owner, my thoughts racing as I mentally assembled a database of plausible deniability. "Nope," I replied in a soft, measured tone, my eyes locking onto his with practiced deception. I had always possessed the uncanny ability to lie to people's faces without the slightest hint of empathy.

"Shoot, maybe it's from a long time ago?" he pondered aloud, his voice trailing off as he spoke. "Can you check in the back room, perhaps in a dusty old corner?" He mumbled to himself, contemplating the odds. "Hmm, I guess realistically it would have been long gone by now... Or, if not, do you have an archive of sold objects?" He seemed lost in his own thoughts. "You see, it was a long time ago when this item was pawned, and I don't know exactly where. You see, it belonged to my grandmother, and upon her death several years ago, all her things were pawned to make some money for the family. But, that candelabra was special, and now that I'm older, I really want to get it back."

Of all the things to be pawned, it had to be that one. How peculiar. I couldn't help but feel a twinge of sympathy for him, knowing that the candelabra was indeed special, but it was now in hands that understood its true significance and would never let it go or reveal its secrets. It was lost to him, as far as I was concerned, and he should abandon his search.

But even with that knowledge, I found myself ensnared in a web of conflicting emotions. On one hand, there was a harsh truth, a reality that I, and I alone, understood. Yet, on the other, there was this man's hope, fragile and flickering like a candle in the wind. I couldn't be the one to snuff it out. With a nonchalant shrug that belied the turmoil inside, my unseen wings flexed, their presence expanding in the room like a silent storm brewing beneath the calm surface. "Sorry, we don't have anything like that here," I repeated, my voice carefully modulated to carry a hint of regret, a subtle echo of the empathy I felt compelled to hide. "I'm truly sorry for your loss." Each word was measured, a careful dance between honesty and the facade I was obliged to maintain.

This man, however, embodied a persistence that seemed as deep-rooted as the ancient trees outside. He wasn't ready to relinquish his quest, not yet, not so easily. With a kind of quiet determination, he continued to survey the shop, his gaze meticulously scanning each shelf and corner, as if hoping to uncover a hidden truth among the relics of others' lives. His eyes, dark and probing, eventually settled on the back door behind me, lingering there with an intensity that spoke of more than just casual curiosity. It was a look that delved, that searched for answers in places unexplored, a look that told me he was accustomed to peering beneath the surface of things. I offered a blunt explanation, "The logs get lost. They don't go farther than five years back."

Finally, his disappointment was evident as he turned away. "Well, alright then. Thank you for your time. If you ever come across anything like I described, could you please ring me at this number?" He extended a slip of paper towards me, his hand steady and purposeful. As I reached out to accept it, our hands nearly brushed, sending an unexpected jolt through me – not of electricity, but of a strange, intangible connection. I quickly retracted into my facade of detachment, letting the paper fall lightly onto the counter. It lay there, a stark white against the dark wood, almost accusing in its simplicity. I glanced at it with feigned disinterest, but inside, a whirlwind of thoughts churned. That piece of paper, with its neatly penned numbers, was more than just a means of contact; it was a symbol of his hope, a tether to a past he yearned to reclaim. In that moment, the shop felt smaller, more confined, as if the walls were closing in on the secret world I had so carefully built.

"Will do," I replied, though my words were devoid of any true intent. Our eyes met briefly, and then he turned and exited the shop. I leaned slightly to the left, my mouth slightly agape, trying to catch a glimpse of him as he walked down the street from the shop window. My left hand gripped the corner of the counter for balance. What an unexpected encounter. I could only hope he wouldn't return to snoop around, but one could never be sure with individuals like him.

I continued with the workday, a lingering sense of unease and anxiety clouding my thoughts. I couldn't shake the fear of what would happen if he ever uncovered my secret. It was a nightmare scenario. People, after all, were not to be trusted. Revealing the truth would spell the end of something extraordinary, and my life would crumble to pieces. What had he been thinking, to come here? Foolish, indeed.

As I continued with the mundane tasks of the day, my nerves still tingling from the unexpected encounter, I couldn't help but dwell on the nature of trust and secrecy. It was a constant undercurrent in my existence, this distrust of the world and its inhabitants. After all, my very being was a living testament to the need for concealment. It wasn't just my clandestine wings, but the dark secrets that resided within my heart.

I pondered the reasons behind my innate negativity, understanding them with a sense of objectivity that had become second nature over the years. Life had taught me the harsh lessons of betrayal and deceit. It had shown me that people, driven by their own desires and ambitions, often pursued their interests at the expense of others. I had witnessed it firsthand, both in my own experiences and through the stories of countless customers who frequented the pawnshop.

To me, trust was a fragile commodity, easily shattered by the whims of fate and human frailty. It was a rarity to find individuals who were truly worthy of it, and even then, one could never be entirely sure. My worldview had been shaped by the shadows and secrets that had become my constant companions. It was in the darkness that I found solace, for there, I could guard my own enigmatic nature.

So, when the man had walked into my shop, seeking something precious that rightfully belonged to him, I couldn't help but view his quest with a sense of cynicism. How foolish, I thought, to place such trust in a world that had shown itself time and again to be untrustworthy. How naive to believe that the past could be rewritten, and that secrets could be unearthed without consequences.

As I continued with the routine tasks of the shop, the feeling that the fragile threads holding my carefully constructed world together were fraying became increasingly persistent. My mind replayed the encounter with the man, each detail etched sharply in my memory. The prospect of my secrets, my true nature, coming to light was a haunting specter that loomed over me. Yet, in the midst of this turmoil, my resolve hardened. I was determined to protect the sanctity of my hidden life, my veiled truths, at any cost. In a world where trust was as elusive and fragile as a shadow, it was the darkness, the quiet anonymity it offered, that had become my steadfast refuge, my greatest ally.

As the day waned and the shop's door closed behind the last customer, I felt a shift within me. The need to immerse myself in the familiar yet mystical world of my own making grew stronger. There was solace in my secret pursuits, a sense of control and freedom that the daylight hours could never offer. With the night's embrace, I prepared to delve into the realms of my hidden passions, to lose myself in the enigmatic dance of spices and spells that awaited me. It was time to retreat into the sanctuary of my own creation, where the mundane faded into the background, and the extraordinary took center stage.

Chapter 6 - Marketplace Enigma

Braids:

Diary entry:

I'm perusing the cinnamon and lavender today, and there's a special selection available. Saffron, a new addition, has piqued my curiosity—I can't wait to see how it will complement my recipes. My notebook hovers above my head, a sentient companion that flits about with the crows, transcribing my thoughts directly into its pages. You see, we share a profound connection, bound by life and a junction spell. It's constructed from black raspberry, citrus chamomile, and all the while, it's been consecrated by the flames of my candelabra. Naturally.

My pockets chime softly, the sound of my treasures jingling as I navigate through the congested pedestrian traffic, bartering and trading my coin for goods. Everyone around me appears so mundane, drab in their gray attire and top hats. Who are these people? They remain oblivious to the world that surrounds them. It's as if they don't see what's right in front of their eyes.

In this labyrinth of gray, I find solace in my peculiar pursuits, an island of curiosity amidst the mundane. And as I delve deeper into the realms of possibility, I can't help but wonder—what other hidden truths lie beneath the surface of this seemingly ordinary world, waiting to be discovered by those who dare to look?

I'm midway through the spice stalls, indulging in the sensory delight of saffron, and relishing the feel of various spices beneath my fingers, much like Amile does. Suddenly, I raise my gaze, and there he stands—what a twisted twist of fate. It's the man from yesterday, the one who had been lurking around my pawnshop, inquiring about my possessions. And now, he's here, standing right before me.

"Ah, Adelia..."

What a nuisance. "Call me Braids," I retort, correcting him. The dandy, the intruder. I wonder if he truly comprehends what he's seeking. One can never be too cautious. I have no idea how much he truly knows about his grandmother, who might have also been a witch.

***

Another day had unfolded in the vibrant town just outside my hometown. It had been about an hour's walk or a swift ten-minute ride on horseback to get there, where the heart of the usually quiet city had pulsed with life—Saturday markets had been the reason. The bustling streets had been filled with the animated presence of men, women, and children, all eager to replenish their shelves and seize a rare bargain. This market had stocked everything, from local treasures to imported wonders.

Colorful silks and linens had beckoned, fresh meat and fruit had beckoned, and raw metal and last year's fashions had awaited. Even homegrown llamas had graced us with their presence. Whatever your heart had desired, it had likely been found there at some point. Yet, discovering those treasures had been a game of chance. Some items had flown off the shelves, while others had remained one-of-a-kind.

Damian's weekly return to those markets had been no doubt driven by the allure of the unexpected and the promise of exotic goods. Herbs and spices, reliable staples, had always beckoned to those seeking to trade.

Curiously, our paths had never crossed before in that crowded marketplace. Perhaps it had been because one didn't tend to notice just another unfamiliar face amidst the bustling crowd. However, once a face had become known, it had had a knack for appearing everywhere you turned, whether you had welcomed it or not.

That day, as always, I had stood by the spice table, gathering my stash of ingredients for both common recipes and the secret spells I had concocted. With one eye perpetually open for new and exotic foreign spices to fuel my candelabra, I had embraced the opportunity to unlock hidden combinations and unseen spells. An old, well-worn ironbound notebook had rested in my pocket, reserved for recording any novel discoveries at the market. This had been distinct from the list I had maintained at home—a catalog brimming with experiments involving those spices.

Saturdays had been my appointed market days, a time to observe the ebb and flow of prices and witness the arrival and departure of potential new ingredients. The shifting seasons had ushered in predictable choices. Yet, I had had to be mindful of my limited coin and resist the temptation to snatch up every novelty in sight.

Patience had been a virtue, and it had often led to more favorable prices in time. But I hadn't been allowed to betray any hint of desperation or excitement when new ingredients had surfaced. If the vendors had caught wind of my consistent purchases, they would have surely exploited the opportunity by inflating their prices. After all, higher perceived value to a customer had equated to higher prices. Thus, I had mastered a few tricks of my own.

One potential approach had involved assuming different identities each week, using a hint of magic to create a myriad of disguises. I had always been alone when I had ventured to the market, but on those leisurely weeks, I could afford to be myself on occasion. Furthermore, I hadn't been obligated to buy from every stall. Competition had naturally driven prices down, and I had played my part by occasionally favoring one vendor over another.

However, there had been a fine balance to maintain. Loyalty could also benefit me, as certain vendors had granted me favorable prices in exchange for consistent patronage. Yet, I had had to ensure that I hadn't always been seen as the eager seeker of every new and exciting thing on offer. It had been a delicate dance of appearances.

One strategy had been to have my alter egos make appearances. As "Braids," I had been a familiar face at Jack's stall, reaping the benefits of a regular arrangement. But if Jack had ever procured something new, I, as "Braids," had had to feign disinterest. Instead, a new persona, "Barbara," might have paid a visit later in the day. Barbara, with her long, curly blonde hair and her attire that had remained a mystery, had been a simple farm girl with a penchant for gardening. She had found delight in experimenting with new spices as plant food.

In the midst of the market's bustling activity, I had pondered the intricacies of my own existence, a solitary island of curiosity amidst a sea of monotony. As I had delved deeper into the potential hidden within these aromatic treasures, I hadn't been able to help but wonder—what other secrets had remained concealed beneath the surface of this ostensibly ordinary world, waiting to be unveiled by those brave enough to seek them?

As I had stood at Jack's stall that day, I had still been "Braids" in the familiar ensemble that had concealed my true identity. Barbara had already scoured the other stalls in search of novelty but had found nothing worth acquiring. However, that day, a new arrival had graced Jack's wares, and Barbara had decided to bide her time. After all, it had been months since regular Braids had bought anything unusual from Jack's collection. Other alter egos of mine had indeed acquired from Jack's oddities in the recent past, but now it had seemed safe for me, in my true form, to employ the trump card—the special prices occasionally bestowed upon familiar customers.

So long as I hadn't revealed my interest too frequently, the tactic should have worked in my favor.

I had examined the selection before me, white-gloved hands on my hips, leaning forward with intent. Adorned in my customary attire—an elegant silky dark blue flowered top hat, a black corset-laced jacket, a frilly black skirt, tights, and black laced-up boots—I had cast my large, discerning eyes over the table once more before meeting the gaze of the stall's owner, Jack. With my body still slightly bent, I had made my choices. "Ten grams of cinnamon, three grams of paprika… a bottle of vanilla… and vegetable oil, please."

Meanwhile, Damian, coincidentally present at the market, had suddenly caught sight of me at the spice table from across the bustling marketplace. He had seized the opportunity to observe me further, his curiosity piqued. It had seemed peculiar, considering his recollections of his grandmother's extensive use of spices, always present for her candelabra. He had decided to approach.

"Hello there, young madam. Do you remember me from the other day, at the pawn shop?" Damian had extended his hand for a second introduction. "I am Damian, by the way." I had acknowledged him with a polite nod and a tip of my hat, then turned to continue my transaction.

Undeterred, Damian had inched closer to the table and initiated a conversation. "You know, it's curious... my grandmother used to buy all kinds of interesting spices here. I would go with her sometimes when I was a boy. She always had a lot around the house. What is it you do with such a vast array, if you don't mind my curiosity?"

Though Damian had tried to appear nonchalant, I couldn't help but feel immensely uncomfortable. This chance encounter, where he had stumbled upon me in the act of buying my ingredients, had been a twist of dumb luck. Yet, I had been well-practiced in crafting alibis for my spice-related habits since childhood. This had been nothing new.

"I just have a fondness for cooking," I had replied with practiced ease. "All kinds, from roast chicken to pastries. Cakes are a real specialty of mine. I dreamt of one day becoming a master and opening up a pastry shop of my own." These had been the generic phrases I had relied on when questioned. They had rolled off my tongue effortlessly, my shield against revealing too much about myself. "I'm here to restock for this week's baking. I buy my spices here because they are the freshest, and I always need to restock. Trying new recipes a lot… really leads one to use up a lot of ingredients."

Damian observed me curiously, attempting to discern any hidden motives or emotions beneath my monotonous voice. Though my face remained concealed, there wasn't much for him to grasp onto.

"With so many experimental dishes going on… there must be loads of cakes and pastries going uneaten then?! My word," he remarked.

I couldn't help but suppress a wry smile. "Well, I would love to stop by and have a taste sometime," Damian proposed.

To maintain appearances, I bowed and cordially curtsied. "Yes, you really should come over some time and taste my baking…" I replied, trying to sound sweet.

"Right then! I shall be seeing you around!" Damian and I arranged a quick exchange of schedule times, agreeing to meet for afternoon tea in the upcoming week. "How exciting," he concluded, winking charmingly before trotting away. There was a noticeable absence of any backward glances or farewell waves from him, but no one could outplay the nonchalant game better than I. To anyone observing, it would seem as though I couldn't care any less. In reality, I was feeling quite smug, confident that this man and his inquisitiveness would soon be out of my hair. Once he tasted my cakes, he would lose all interest in me and my candelabra.

The spice table's owner was accustomed to my peculiar demeanor. I had been a loyal customer for years, and he knew from personal experience that I was, indeed, a great baker. I had even brought him some cake in the past—a gesture that most would perceive as sweet, a token of gratitude for the ingredients. However, in my unusual mind, it served a different purpose. It was my way of allaying the paranoia that people didn't believe my story. During my adolescence, I struggled to understand others' thoughts, their knowledge that differed from my own—an aspect of "theory of mind." So, as a young girl, I baked and handed out cakes to anyone in my life, creating a diversion that no one was following and ridding myself of surplus homemade cake.

The spice stall owner saw nothing peculiar in my interaction with the peculiar newcomer. In fact, he commented that Damian seemed a bit odd. I couldn't help but snort in agreement. "Thank you! I'm glad somebody gets it!" With that, I lifted my hands, clapping them together before paying for my groceries and casually walking away.

Chapter 7 - Beneath the Surface

Braids:

I stood there, eyeing a beaker of water placed delicately on the kitchen counter. Exactly one cup, perfect. I raised myself from its level, one hand on my hip, the other crooked and pressed up to my mouth. The question lingered—would it be cookies or a cake for Damian? He struck me as more of a cookies kind of guy. I sighed and poured the water into the mix I'd prepared earlier, stirring it by hand.

That afternoon, I planned to surprise him with these treats. If he doubted my culinary skills, I had to prove him wrong. After all, what other reason could there be for my extensive collection of spices? Baking had always been my way of covering up my secret. He would be no challenge.

Each time I baked, I had to make up for the spices used somehow. I needed all the spices I bought for my spells, so how did I also afford to use them for cooking? Spells, of course! Once all the ingredients were in the mixing bowl, I sprinkled some enhanced, magically burnt cinnamon into the candelabra. Then, I continued to hand-stir vigorously, and the dough gradually increased in quantity. I placed the dough in a round pan and instead of putting it in the oven, I employed a spell to ignite my hand and set the cake ablaze. The flame burned blue for a moment, soaking into the cake somehow. Then, it was fully absorbed, and the delightful aroma of freshly baked cake filled the air. The surface of the cake appeared crisp and golden brown. I smiled and nodded with pride at my success.

Soon, there was a knock at the door. I hurried out of the kitchen, wiping my flaming hands on my soft linen black skirt until they appeared normal again. With a smile on my face and my best shine in my eye, I opened the door and let Damian in.

"Hello, Braids. I hope your afternoon is going well," he greeted me, tapping his hat politely before removing it and placing it, along with his jacket, on a coat rack. I led him to the living room, where I had already arranged the tea cups and only needed to fetch the steaming pot of tea sitting on the wood-burning stove in the kitchen.

Damian took a seat on one of the two couches, which faced each other. His eyes remained fixed on mine, and a bright smile adorned his face. "So, welcome to my little home," I said, injecting mock enthusiasm as I poured the scalding tea for both of us.

"I hope I don't trouble you with this visit."

"What is your name again, sir?" I pretended not to know.

"My name is Damian."

"And what do you do for a living?" I said as I left the room to bring the cake. In the kitchen, I held my hand over the circular cake. At that moment, eight even slices appeared, perfectly cut from the center.

"I'm a pianist for the local philharmonic. We have big concerts a few times a year, but most of the time I play smaller gigs in town to pick up some extra money. It's not easy to make a living as a musician, you know. Must be interesting working in the pawn shop, seeing all kinds of interesting things come through here."

"No, it's really not. Just a bunch of annoying customers buying junk from a junk shop. Asking me dumb questions.

The best is when they just browse quietly, or just buy something and get out."

"Oh wow, this is amazing," he said, tasting the cake. "Did you bake this yourself?"

"Yes, I like to bake."

"I see."

There was an awkward pause.

"So, what do you do for a living?" Damian returned the question.

"I work in my father's shop..."

"Right." Damian looked down at his tea and stirred it. "Anyway, what I actually came here to tell you about was a bit of family history. I came in here the other day looking for a candelabra. My grandmother's. She passed away some years ago, and upon her death, my mother wanted nothing to do with her and threw away all her stuff, and pawned some of the others. I was only a small child then, but I remember a lot about my grandmother and that her candelabra was very special to her. It is, therefore, very special to me, and I have come seeking it all around this city and the general cities around our village."

My heart raced as I watched my father's intrusion into my life, bringing it to a screeching halt. The heat of anger and embarrassment flushed my cheeks, making me wish I could vanish into the shadows. Damian's untimely visit had already turned this encounter into an unbearable nightmare, and now my father was becoming a part of it.

"Hello there, sir," my father greeted Damian politely, unaware of the turmoil he was causing in my world. "Welcome to our home. Sorry to interrupt, but, Braids, I just wanted to talk to you about the schedule and your next shift for the store. I will be going across town for a dental appointment now, but I see you are busy, so I will let you be and close up for now."

Suppressing my frustration, I bit my lip until it hurt. I couldn't believe Damian had chosen such an inconvenient time to visit me, and now my father was tangled up in this already awkward situation.

"Excuse me," Damian said apologetically before excusing himself. I nodded weakly and pointed down the hall to indicate the restroom. As Damian walked away, my sigh of relief was accompanied by a surge of anger. I was furious at both of them for disrupting my life.

Damian, however, had other plans in mind. Instead of heading to the restroom, he diverted from his course, closing the restroom door while standing outside it. He then continued down the back steps and entered the unlocked, closed pawn shop. Panic washed over me as I realized he was nosing around where he shouldn't be, dangerously close to uncovering my secret.

As I watched him from the doorway, my heart pounded like a drum. Every second felt like an eternity. I couldn't comprehend why he was taking such liberties, invading my sanctuary without a second thought.

He began to search the shop, likely hoping to find the candelabra in the back room. My frustration and anxiety grew with each passing moment, my anger directed squarely at Damian for his intrusive behavior.

He quickly discovered the archives, a log of all items bought and sold over the years. I clenched my fists, my anger boiling over as I watched him flip through our records, uninvited and unwelcome.

I prayed he wouldn't find anything incriminating. The dread hung heavy in the air as Damian reached the final page, which happened to be blank. My frustration reached its peak as he tampered with our records, crumpling the blank page into a ball and placing it at the top of a shelf near the entrance to the main pawn shop.

With his plan in place, Damian returned upstairs to rejoin our meeting, leaving me seething with anger and frustration. My carefully constructed life had been recklessly disrupted, and I couldn't help but resent him for it.

***

Braids:

In the dimly lit kitchen, my journal lurked on a high shelf in the pantry, diligently recording my thoughts, unfazed by my grumpy disposition.

"This should settle things," I muttered, squeezing the last swirls of frosting onto the exquisite cupcakes I had been meticulously preparing for the past hour. The aroma of tea wafted through the air, signaling Damian's imminent arrival. I knew he would be here soon, and I couldn't help but frown at the intrusion into my carefully guarded world.

I continued to work on the batter, my gloved hands moving with practiced precision. The mixture took on a velvety texture, each ingredient blending seamlessly into the other. My eyes bore into the bowl, scrutinizing every nuance, every subtle transformation, a grumble escaping my lips. I couldn't deny that, despite my irritation, there was a certain satisfaction in the artistry of baking.

As I labored, the Flow began to take hold, its grasp unrelenting. It was an inexplicable sensation, one that defied rationalization. My thoughts dissipated, leaving only the vivid awareness of the present moment. I felt every inch of my human body, from the delicate dance of my individual toes across the wooden floor to the gentle embrace of my fingertips around the spatula. It was as if I were a wide-eyed child, captivated by the sheer wonder of existence.

The world around me faded into insignificance as the power of creation surged through me. Whether I held a paintbrush or a spatula, it didn't matter; the possibilities were boundless. I was merely a vessel, my subconscious mind dictating what was right and what would come to be. It was a phenomenon that defied the boundaries of human understanding.

In that transcendent moment, the desire and frustration that often accompanied the quest to create something extraordinary dissipated. I was no longer the architect of my work; I was a conduit, channeling inspiration from the depths of the cosmos. It whispered to me, guiding my hands with divine intent, and I surrendered to its influence.

When the act of creation reached its culmination, I couldn't help but celebrate the masterpiece that had come into being through my hands. It was an odd paradox—I owned it, and yet I marveled at it, for it felt as if it had originated from somewhere beyond myself, a gift from the universe.

The mournful howl of a bloodhound pierced the air from outside, and I knew that it had caught sight of Damian approaching. The hound often perched itself near the cemetery across the street, serving as a peculiar, enchanted sentinel that alerted me to any visitors ascending our stoop.

I hesitated, resisting the urge to approach the door. To show too much anticipation would be beneath me. I couldn't afford to place my trust in fate or people, allowing them to catch me by surprise.

The bloodhound's mournful howl resounded once more, and shortly thereafter, the man—Damian—rapped on my door. He removed his elegant top hat and executed a low bow, adhering to social conventions. Suppressing a sigh, I curtseyed in return, my eyes involuntarily rolling at the formality of it all. His petticoat was visible behind him, a detail I took in without much interest.

"Please, do come in, sir," I said sweetly, leading him into the parlor room. He took a seat, expressing his gratitude. "Tea will be ready shortly."

Our gazes locked as I set down the silver tray adorned with cupcakes, two tea cups, and a cake—all masterfully crafted with a multitude of spices. He savored a bite of the delectable treat, uttering an appreciative sound.

I hadn't lied; my skills as a baker were unparalleled. Concealing my true self and my magical abilities had become second nature to me. I had been hiding my spells even from Aunt Biddie throughout my life, a necessity that had led me to take up baking in the first place. Besides, between my tutoring lessons and the baked goods I offered, it was an effective means of silencing curiosity. Once one's sweet tooth was satisfied and content, one tended not to pry further.

He seemed thoroughly pleased with the cupcakes, a gratifying outcome. Later, when he took his leave, I decided it was time to investigate him further.

"You absolutely must attend my show next week," he insisted, handing me a flyer for his upcoming piano concert before departing.

Chapter 8 - Invisible Echoes of Enchantment

Braids:

The invitation to Damian's piano concert had piqued my curiosity, but I wasn't one to venture into unknown territory without proper preparation. New environments and crowds tended to unnerve me, so I needed to ensure that I wouldn't be caught off guard.

I decided it was high time to gather more information about this Damian character.

"One ticket to the upcoming piano concert, please," I said, peering into the glossy window of the ticket booth. The ticket seller, dressed in a sharp red uniform, gave an exasperated sigh before quoting the price. "Ten pounds."

His impeccable red suit clashed significantly with his complete lack of charm as a theater ticket vendor. It was a puzzling choice for individuals in such uninspiring roles within the grand hierarchy of the theater. Perhaps it was an attempt to compensate for their otherwise dreary dispositions, providing a veneer of charm to the otherwise mundane task of ticket sales.

I handed over the ten pounds, accepting the ticket without much fanfare, and promptly stashed it in my pocket before distancing myself from the booth.

I navigated the grimy streets, avoiding the curious glances of my fellow citizens until I reached the bar where I met my spectral companions. I took a swig of my cinnamon shot, sauntered around the corner to the dimly lit section near the restrooms, and before long, I found myself upsidedown, feet on the ceiling.

I hung upside down from the ceiling of the dimly lit bar, my spectral form hovering above a table where my ghostly companions engaged in a timeless poker game. They were the only friends I had, the only ones who truly understood my peculiar predicament.

"Deal me in," I announced, sliding into the transparent chair amid their incorporeal forms.

The ghosts exchanged knowing glances as they shuffled the ethereal deck of cards. They tried to offer me insights into my ongoing situation with Damian and his persistent attempts to buy back the candelabra that rightfully belonged to me. It was mine, imbued with powerful magic, and I had no intention of parting with it. Keeping my secret safe was paramount, and I certainly didn't want Damian to discover my possession of the precious artifact.

As we played through the rounds of poker, they offered tips and advice, their wispy voices filled with concern. But in the end, their well-intentioned counsel proved to be of little use.

"Come on, Braids, you should just give it back," one of the ghosts urged, lacking the resolve to understand the importance of my connection to the candelabra.

I scowled and shook my head. "No way, it's mine, and he can't have it."

Another ghost chimed in, "But you could make a deal, get something in return..."

I interrupted, my voice tinged with irritation, "No deals. That candelabra is too precious to me."

The Gemool were well-meaning, but their advice was tinged with cowardice. I needed to protect my secrets, and I wouldn't let anyone, even Damian, jeopardize that.

So The Gemool were little help.

***

That night, I descended into the labyrinthine underground and made my way to the venue where Damian was set to perform. The dark and winding tunnels of the underground always put me on edge, but I endured the discomfort, knowing that I needed to see Damian's performance up close.

The crowd in the theater was bustling and adorned in fancy clothing that made me feel even more out of place. I settled into a seat in the third row, next to the grand piano, ensuring that nobody else occupied the first three rows. I preferred to keep my distance from the chattering masses.

Before the show began, a couple in the fourth row struck up a conversation with me, claiming they knew Damian from church and spoke highly of him. They asked if I knew him as well, and I replied curtly that we were "sorta friends." In truth, I knew Damian only on a superficial level, but the couple seemed oblivious to that fact.

As the show started, the spotlight focused on Damian, and the surrounding darkness engulfed me. It felt as if there were no one else in the room except him and me. He couldn't see me, hidden in the shadows, as he played his enchanting melodies. When the performance concluded, I discreetly slipped away from the theater, avoiding the after-show meet-and-greet.

Outside, the brisk wind rustled my dark attire as I stretched my wings and walked away with flames dancing on my fingertips.

On another night, I returned to the venue, this time taking a seat near the front right side with an unobstructed view of the piano. The first several rows around me remained vacant, which was precisely what I had hoped for. However, within the next half-hour, more spectators trickled in, and the surrounding seats gradually filled up. My solitude was disrupted when an elderly couple settled down almost directly behind me.

I tried to block out their murmured conversation, but their words were still audible.

"Oh yes, Damian is certainly wonderful! I do love his music. What a sweet boy!"

"I know, he plays so charmingly on Sundays at church."

Their words made me blush. Someone was speaking kindly of that nosy Damian. Unable to resist, I turned around, wondering if I could glean any useful information from this unexpected source.

"Excuse me," I interjected, "are you talking about the piano player?"

The elderly woman smiled warmly, "Why yes, Damian. He plays the piano for us at church! Such a lovely man."

"I see," I replied, feigning interest.

The elderly man joined in, "And how do you know him?"

I hesitated for a moment, then reluctantly revealed, "Oh, just from around town."

The elderly couple seemed intrigued, and the woman commented, "Well, you would be a lucky girl, then."

I blushed even deeper, flustered by their assumptions. "Oh! Not like that! Just...business. He was a customer once."

I instantly regretted sharing that tidbit of information, but the couple's presence had already begun to grate on my nerves. They had interrupted my moment of peace and solitude, and I couldn't wait to be rid of their prying questions.

I sat there, growing increasingly agitated by the incessant chatter of the elderly couple behind me. Their prying questions and their adoration for Damian were beginning to gnaw at my patience. I needed them to stop talking to me. An idea formed in my mind, and I decided to use my magic to make them forget I was even there.

Drawing upon my magical abilities, I subtly began to weave a spell. My fingers moved discreetly under the table, tracing invisible sigils in the air. I invoked the incantation softly, and a subtle shimmer enveloped the elderly couple, almost like a gentle haze.

As I continued to murmur the incantation, I directed the magic to target their memories. It was a delicate process, one that required precision and finesse. My spell wove its way into their consciousness, nudging at their memories of our encounter.

Slowly but surely, their voices began to trail off, their sentences fading into vague mumbles. The elderly woman's smile faltered as her eyes lost focus, and the elderly man blinked, clearly disoriented.

Their gazes drifted past me, as though I had become invisible, and their attention turned back to the empty stage. It was working; my magic was erasing me from their perception.

With a final flourish of my fingers, I completed the spell, ensuring that the couple would remember nothing about our conversation or my presence. They were now lost in a fog of forgetfulness, their minds blissfully unaware of my existence.

Relieved that I had silenced them, I returned my focus to the stage, content in the knowledge that I could now enjoy the rest of the performance in peace.

The stage darkened, creating a dramatic ambiance that sent a hush through the audience. The room's atmosphere seemed to hold its breath in anticipation as the stage gradually filled with a large choir, elegantly dressed in matching black suits and dresses. A ripple of applause rippled through the audience, a sign of their excitement and appreciation.

And then, he appeared.

Damian walked onto the stage with a confident yet humble demeanor. He acknowledged the applause with a graceful bow before taking his seat at the grand piano. The audience's enthusiasm grew, their applause now mixed with whispers of admiration.

I watched him intently from my vantage point, hidden in the shadows. His hands, elegant and skilled, glided over the piano keys, fingers dancing with precision and grace. The melodies he conjured were both enchanting and haunting, filling the air with a mesmerizing symphony.

On the conductor's cue, a thin, balding man in a flowing black suit, complete with tails, waved his conductor's wand. The choir, standing behind Damian, began to sing in harmonious unison. Their voices blended seamlessly, creating a hauntingly beautiful backdrop to Damian's piano performance.

As Damian played on, lost in the music, it was as if the entire world had faded away. The audience was captivated, their eyes fixed on the stage, their hearts moved by the exquisite performance unfolding before them. And in that moment, hidden in the darkness, I couldn't deny that there was indeed a magnetic charm to Damian's music, a power that drew everyone under its spell. Pun aside.

He played on...

The music, Damian's music, enveloped the room like a living, breathing entity. It was as if the very air around us had become charged with an otherworldly energy, and I couldn't escape its enchantment. The haunting melodies flowed from the piano and the choir, weaving a mesmerizing tapestry that held the entire audience captive.

I felt myself drawn into the music, my grumpy exterior slowly melting away as the enchantment of the performance took hold. It was a moment beyond time, beyond the mundane world I was so accustomed to. In that instant, it was as though it was just Damian and me, lost in a shared reverie, playing for each other's souls.

My senses were heightened, every note, every chord, resonated within me. I could feel the music coursing through my veins, my heart beating in rhythm with the piano's keys. The world outside the theater ceased to exist; all that mattered was the magic unfolding on the stage.

Damian's fingers danced across the piano with effortless grace, each note a declaration of his passion and skill. The choir's voices soared, a haunting symphony that echoed in the depths of my soul. It was a moment of pure, unadulterated magic, and I was completely spellbound.

As the final notes hung in the air, time seemed to stand still. The audience erupted into thunderous applause, their cheers and ovations a testament to the profound impact of the performance. But for me, in that moment, I was frozen in place, held captive by the sheer beauty and power of the music.

It was a fantastical experience, a breathtaking moment that I hadn't expected. The grumpy exterior I so often wore had been stripped away, and for that brief interlude, I had been transported to a world of magic and wonder. Damian's music had touched my heart, leaving an indelible mark on my soul.

Halfway through the performance, I felt an irresistible urge to get closer to the source of this enchanting music. My grumpiness had long since melted away, and the magic of the performance had me in its thrall. With a thought, I dialed up the invisibility spell I had cast earlier, my hands shimmering with a ghostly, twinkling blue light. I became ethereal, a mere whisper in the darkness, invisible to the enraptured crowd.

I floated towards the stage, moving like a wraith in the dimly lit theater. My feet didn't touch the ground; instead, I glided effortlessly up the steps, drawn to the pianist's side. There, I witnessed the true magic of the evening.

Damian's fingers moved furiously across the piano keys, a blur of motion and grace. His hands, sleek and elegant with long, slender fingers, were a sight to behold. They danced and fluttered across the keys with incredible speed, creating a symphony of sound that illuminated and enchanted my very soul.

It was as if his hands possessed a magic of their own, a power that transcended the mundane world. Each note he played held a piece of his heart, and I could feel the raw emotion pouring forth from the piano. I was captivated, completely lost in the music and the mesmerizing sight before me.

As I hovered invisibly by his side, I couldn't help but marvel at the beauty of his performance. It was a moment of pure, unadulterated magic, and I felt privileged to be so close to the source. The world around us faded into obscurity, and for that fleeting moment, it was just Damian, his piano, and the invisible girl who had been transformed by the power of his music.

I couldn't resist the urge to get even closer to Damian. His face, so captivating from a distance, drew me in like a moth to a flame. My ethereal form allowed me to approach without disturbing him, and I peered into his face with a newfound intimacy.

His long, thin nose, which might have seemed ordinary from afar, was now charming and distinctive on that handsome face. His eyes, oh, those eyes burned with an intensity I hadn't fully appreciated before. They were like twin flames, flickering with passion and purpose as he continued to play, his fingers moving with lightning speed across the keys.

The music that flowed from his piano was like smoke, rising and enveloping us in its ethereal embrace. I tried to remain composed, to not be swept away by the enchantment of the moment. Every note, every chord seemed to resonate with my very soul.

Turning my gaze away from Damian, I surveyed the audience. Many were equally enchanted, leaning forward in their seats, their eyes fixed on the pianist as if under a spell. It felt as if the entire world had been transported to this magical realm created by Damian's music. Even a stone monster, guarding the very pits of hell, would have been moved by the beauty and emotion of this performance. It was a moment that transcended the ordinary and reached into the realm of the extraordinary, and I was fortunate to be a part of it, even if only in my invisible form.

Chapter 9 - Ethereal Currents and Unseen Threads

Braids:

After the concert, I had no interest in the post-performance mingling. I didn't crave their muffins or idle chatter. The music had left me drained, and I longed for solitude to immerse myself in the lingering echoes of the piano's melody. With wings outstretched, I soared home on the ethereal currents and alighted on my rooftop.

Oh, what has happened to me?

I collapsed onto my bed, exhaustion pulling me into slumber, but my dreams offered no respite. In the vivid recesses of my mind, I saw Damian, seated peacefully on his bed, engrossed in a book. The dream was surreal, each detail as clear as the light of day. Initially, I observed from above, but soon I became a mouse, scurrying about his room with an inexplicable sense of unease.

The floor felt uncomfortable, filled with the looming threat of a careless step that could crush a mouse's existence. I needed a safer vantage point and scaled the bed's foot. There, I surveyed Damian, my paws aligned for balance. Unaware of my presence, he continued to read. My curiosity propelled me closer, onto the bedding, near his feet.

Tension gripped the dream as Damian sensed my tiny presence. He looked up from his book, his gaze locking onto mine. With book in hand, he lowered it onto his lap, a gesture signaling his willingness to engage with the inexplicable. In the charged atmosphere, still on my hands and knees, I transformed, rising to my feet as our eyes remained fixed upon each other.

We both seemed startled yet intrigued. Slowly, I raised my hand, poised to snap my fingers and teleport myself out of this bewildering dream. Damian, somehow aware of my intent, whispered a quiet, "no, don't." My hand froze in mid-air, and I withdrew it slowly, my gaze never leaving his. I crawled closer, and he welcomed me onto his lap.

Our encounter became passionate, with kisses and embraces, gradually leading to the removal of clothing. The dream grew hazy and intense.

I woke with a start, bewildered and disgusted by the vivid, unexpected turn of events. It was a dream so outlandish, it shook me to my core. A faint glimmer of doubt crossed my mind, suggesting that perhaps Damian wasn't as nefarious as I'd believed. Could he even be befriended?

The thought of sharing my knowledge of the candelabra with him flitted through my mind, but I quickly dismissed it as preposterous. Yet, despite my inner protests, a longing to connect with another human being lingered. Maybe, just maybe, we could be friends.

To clear my head and contemplate my newfound feelings, I decided to leave the house for a long walk in the park. It was the perfect time for some magical experiments, a distraction from the turmoil within.

Braids:

Things appeared brighter, even the ravens took on an unusual pallor. Alright, I admit it, I had cast a spell. I let out a heavy sigh; it seemed my grasp on sanity was slipping, and I couldn't deny the peculiar craving that had come over me. It was like a wolf, ravenous and fixated, but not on sheep, mind you; don't let your illusions be shattered. The notion that wolves primarily prey on sheep is a biased human perspective.

But I digress. Where was I?

Abruptly, the sensation washed over me, and I found myself snapping out of it. I sat on the ground, legs stretched out, my hands firmly locked and tucked beneath my thighs. A rapid series of fluttering blinks followed as I shook off the strange trance. My eyes, once fixated on the distant trees, slowly returned to normal, their dilated pupils shrinking back to their usual size.

Why did he affect me this way, so profoundly different from anyone else? More than I could have ever imagined. My heart continued to race, but I managed to take a deep, satisfying breath. I darted my eyes around, shifting my attention to the surrounding trees.

The sun had disappeared from the sky, leaving my earlier campfire as the main source of illumination. I couldn't afford to forget the way out of here. I knew I needed a good night's sleep for the journey ahead, but my thoughts clung to me, keeping my attention through the night.

I lay on my roof, gazing at the stars.

Maybe, just maybe, I should consider showing him the candelabra. Perhaps things could turn out alright.

Isn't it remarkable how many things surround us, just within the reach of our senses, that often go unnoticed because our minds simply don't know how to process them? The vividness of colors, the intricate textures of objects, the incredible details we could observe if only we paid closer attention. It's like those breathtaking professional photographs we come across on the internet every day, waiting for someone to appreciate them. But we don't... until certain moments in life arrive.

Moments like sadness, a simple and unexplainable happiness, or love. Those times when everything feels right, when life takes on an artistic quality, and every detail demands our attention, like watching a well-crafted movie.

I went for a walk a few days ago, and my mind was buzzing with awareness. I noticed the distinct angles of leaves on plants and keenly felt the warmth of the sun on my skin. It was as though I had entered a fantasy world, but it was all inside me. I became acutely aware of colors—vibrant red leaves with intricate green veins, crushed beneath my toes and radiating warmth through my thin leather shoe. My eyes darted and captured the knots on tree trunks as I walked past them, their rough bark forming intricate patterns of brown spikes. Tiny, dewy leaves embraced the gnarled branches of distant, scraggly trees, each tree with its own unique character.

Even the ground was adorned with autumn-colored leaves, despite the fact that it was spring. Non-native trees created a perpetual state of natural wonder, fascinating both animals and observant humans alike.

Lately, my life has been like walking through a dream, each moment infused with an ethereal quality, as if I were both a participant and an observer in a beautifully crafted movie. This surreal experience, while mesmerizing, often leaves me feeling detached, like a spectator unable to fully immerse herself in the storyline. There's a certain frustration in experiencing such beauty and complexity, yet feeling unable to retain and comprehend it all. My human limitations stand stark against the vivid tapestry of life that unfolds around me.

Carrying this sense of surreal disconnection with me, I found myself once again in the dimly lit ambiance of the bar. It was as if the bar, with its shadowy corners and murmurs of conversation, was a continuation of the dreamlike state in which I'd been living. Here, the boundaries between the real and the unreal seemed blurred, making it the perfect place to reconnect with the Gemool.

In the pocket of my coat, hidden from curious eyes, was a small vial containing a shimmering potion. I glanced around, ensuring I was unnoticed, and quickly drank the mysterious liquid. The effect was immediate and disorienting, yet familiar. The world around me turned upside down, an apt metaphor for the way I'd been feeling. As gravity reversed its pull, I felt myself being lifted towards the ceiling, which now served as a peculiar floor.

This transition, from the ordinary to the extraordinary, seemed a natural progression from the dreamlike state of my recent days. In this inverted world, I sought the counsel of the Gemool, hoping their ghostly wisdom could help me navigate the complexities and frustrations of my life, both seen and unseen.

As I approached the Gemool's poker table, suspended in this inverted realm, their ghostly figures acknowledged my arrival. The ethereal cards shuffled in their translucent hands, a surreal scene amidst the mundane backdrop of the bar.

"I need to understand what's happening to me," I said, my voice tinged with a mix of confusion and curiosity. The Gemool, with their age-old wisdom, turned their hollow gazes upon me.

"You're developing feelings for Damian," one of them stated, his voice echoing as if from a deep well. It was a simple statement, but it hit me with the force of a revelation.

The realization brought a mix of emotions. Part of me felt a surge of hope, envisioning a future where everything could work out, where I could be 'Happy Braids,' free from the shadows that usually clung to me. The idea of a solution, a narrative with Damian that ended in happiness, began to take shape in my mind.

But as I sat among the Gemool, I couldn't help but feel a twinge of frustration. I looked at them, these specters of the past, and saw their eternal hesitation, their fear of taking action in life. "You always played it safe, never daring to chase what you truly wanted," I found myself saying, a note of chastisement in my tone.

The Gemool seemed to ponder this, their ghostly forms flickering like old film. They were a mirror to my own fears – the fear of reaching out, of embracing the possibilities of life and love. Sitting there, in this upside-down world, I realized that I didn't want to end up like them, trapped in eternal regret.

I needed to face my feelings for Damian, to confront the possibilities head-on, no matter how frightening they seemed. The Gemool, with their silent, knowing stares, had given me the answer I needed. It was time to leave the comfort of shadows and step into the uncertain light of the living world.

***

Later that evening, I was in the basement of our home, a space I had claimed as my own for magical experiments and solitude. The faint sound of footsteps on the stairs pulled me from my thoughts. It was my father, Jean-Louis, holding an envelope in his hand.

"Braids, this came for you," he said, handing me the letter. His expression was one of mild curiosity, always intrigued by the occasional oddities that my life seemed to attract.

I took the envelope, noting the formal handwriting on the front. My name was elegantly scripted, and as I opened it, a sense of anticipation washed over me. Inside was an invitation, embossed and formal, from Damian. It was an invite to one of his shows. A surge of mixed emotions ran through me. He didn't know I had already seen him perform, a secret observer in his audience.

"Did a man named Damian come by the shop recently?" I asked my father, trying to mask the urgency in my voice.

"Yes, a few days ago," he replied, scratching his head. "Nice fellow. Seemed very keen on finding out if we had a certain candelabra. Why do you ask?"

So, he was the one who had come asking about the candelabra. My mind raced, piecing together his actions and my own experiences. He was on my trail, and I needed to be one step ahead. I pondered over the invitation, seeing it as both an opportunity and a risk.

"I was just curious," I replied nonchalantly, trying to keep my composure. I couldn't let my father know the depth of the situation. He would worry, and I didn't want to add to his burdens.

After my father left, I sat in the basement, the invitation in hand, lost in thought. I needed a plan to throw Damian off my trail, to keep my magical life separate from whatever intentions he had. It was a delicate game of cat and mouse, and I had to play it wisely.

The invitation sat on my worktable, a symbol of the intricate dance that was unfolding in my life. I needed to be cautious, to think through each move carefully. In the world of magic and secrets, one wrong step could unravel everything I had worked so hard to protect.

Chapter 10 - Melodies

Braids:

As I settled into my seat at the concert hall, the anticipation of Damian's performance hung in the air. The atmosphere was charged with excitement, and I could feel the collective energy of the audience humming around me. The music was about to transport us all to another world.

Once again, as Damian's fingers gracefully glided over the piano keys, I felt myself being swept away by the enchanting melodies. It was as if the very notes he played had a life of their own, reaching out to embrace each one of us in the audience.

I couldn't help but be drawn to his side once more, invisible to the rest of the world, my eyes fixated on his hands as they danced across the keys. The music swirled around me, enveloping me in a whirlwind of emotions. Each note resonated within me, stirring feelings I had long buried.

It was a sensation unlike any other, a feeling of being both grounded and weightless, as if I were floating on a sea of melodies. I was caught in a rapture, a beautiful cacophony of emotions and sensations that filled every corner of my being.

As the performance continued, I couldn't help but wonder what had brought this magic into my life. What had changed? The answers remained elusive, hidden in the depths of the music that now surrounded me, wrapping me in its ethereal embrace.

The concert ended, and as the lights came on, I knew I had to rejoin the crowd to find Damian in the post-concert chaos.

Something inside me compelled me to see him, to be acknowledged by him. I couldn't deny that there was an excitement building within me, an anticipation I had never experienced before. My heart raced, and my teeth chattered with nervous energy, an unusual sensation for someone like me who usually kept her emotions tightly under control.

I wove my way through the colorful sea of people spilling out of the concert hall, a mixture of ladies in extravagant dresses and gentlemen in sleek black suits. It was a whirl of scents and sights, and I couldn't help but feel a strange sense of urgency to find him.

"Adelia!" A voice called out above the din, and I turned my head to locate its source. There he was, a head taller than most in the crowd. We closed the distance between us, our hands locking in the crooks of each other's arms as if we were old friends. It was a formal gesture, meant to convey a sense of politeness, but the warm pulsing waves that shot up my arm at his touch took me by surprise. No, I told myself, someone like him could not possibly make me feel this way.

"Adelia, I'm so glad you came! You're my special guest of honor," Damian exclaimed with a smile that was both charming and corny. I scowled inwardly, my heart fluttering in a way I couldn't control. Despite my inner turmoil, I managed to put on a polite smile.

The scene continued to unfold as Damian introduced me to his girlfriend, and a pang of jealousy surged through me. I tried to hide it, but it gnawed at me from within, and I couldn't help but wonder why I felt this way. Damian's girlfriend was lovely, and yet, I couldn't shake the feeling of possessiveness that had taken hold of me.

As Damian introduced me to his girlfriend, Rosalie, I felt a sharp pang of jealousy bubbling up inside me. I couldn't quite put my finger on why I felt this way, but it gnawed at me from within, like a persistent itch I couldn't scratch. Damian's girlfriend, Rosalie, was undeniably lovely, with her radiant smile and graceful demeanor.

"Adelia, this is Rosalie," Damian said, his voice warm and welcoming. "Rosalie, this is Adelia, a friend of mine from town."

Rosalie extended her hand toward me with a friendly smile. "It's a pleasure to meet you, Adelia. Damian has told me so much about you."

I shook her hand, my own smile feeling forced. "Likewise, Rosalie. Damian has mentioned you as well."

The conversation flowed on, with Damian and Rosalie sharing stories about their recent travels and experiences. They seemed so genuinely happy together, and the contrast between their easy camaraderie and my own sense of jealousy only intensified my inner turmoil.

I couldn't help but glance at Damian when he wasn't looking, my eyes studying the way he looked at Rosalie, the fondness in his gaze. It was as if they were in their own little world, and I felt like an intruder.

As the evening wore on, I realized that I needed to get a grip on my emotions. This was foolish, I thought, as I tried to push aside the possessiveness that had taken hold of me. Damian was not mine to claim, and I had no right to feel this way about his relationship with Rosalie. Yet, the more I tried to suppress my jealousy, the more it seemed to consume me.

***

Perhaps my life was mundane before, but there was a certain contentment in its simplicity. My needs were met, my days predictable. However, everything changed when I stumbled upon this new, hidden realm. It was as if a torch had been thrown into an ancient tomb, illuminating the darkness, revealing secrets and histories I never knew existed. Now, I find myself unable to live without that light, that revelation of a world beyond the ordinary.

This place, this hidden corner of existence, is not one many know of, let alone enter. It has become my secret sanctuary, a place I escape to whenever the opportunity arises. My everyday life pales in comparison to the call of this wondrous realm. I find myself willing to drop everything at a moment's notice, summoned by its allure.

But I was wrong about the outside world; it's even more decrepit than I had initially thought. In a moment of spite, I burnt all the flowers in the park, so he couldn't enjoy them. Why did I do it? I suppose it was a reaction to what happened next.

I attended his play, this time as an invited guest. The theater was bustling, more crowded than before. His performance was enchanting, just as it had been the first time. After the show, amidst the throng of people, I spotted him. Our eyes locked, and for a moment, everything else faded away.

I approached him, heart pounding, ready to express my admiration for his music. But as I poured out my feelings, making myself vulnerable, he introduced me to a redheaded woman by his side — his fiancée. The shock, the embarrassment of that moment was overwhelming. I struggled to maintain my composure, playing along just long enough to make a graceful exit.

Fleeing the theater, I dashed into the streets, finding solace in a dark alleyway. There, I allowed my true self to emerge. My wings, usually hidden, unfurled in the darkness, their ashen black feathers a stark contrast to the night sky. I took to the air, soaring back to the safety of my rooftop.

In that flight, there was a release, a freedom from the constraints of the world below. But it was also an escape from the pain of unrequited feelings and the harsh reality of human relationships. The world I had once found dull yet comforting now seemed harsh and unforgiving. And yet, the hidden realm I had discovered, with its magical allure, remained a constant, a place where I could find solace and a sense of belonging.

Chapter 11 - Levitation

Damian:

I had been following her for some time, this enigmatic girl named Braids. There was something about her, something otherworldly that piqued my curiosity. So, when she entered the bar, I trailed behind, careful to keep a discreet distance.

The bar was dimly lit, a haven for those seeking solace in the shadows. I watched Braids as she made her way through the crowd, an air of mystery enveloping her. She seemed to move with a purpose, her eyes scanning the room before settling on a particular spot.

What happened next defied explanation. Braids reached into her pocket, pulling out something small and inconspicuous. She took it swiftly, and then, to my utter disbelief, her feet left the ground. She ascended gracefully, as if pulled by invisible strings, towards the ceiling. The sight was so surreal, so utterly impossible, that I blinked several times, convinced my eyes were deceiving me.

But there she was, defying gravity, moving along the ceiling with an ease that was both beautiful and terrifying. The patrons below remained oblivious, engrossed in their drinks and conversations, unaware of the spectacle unfolding above them.

As I watched, rooted to the spot in shock, Braids suddenly vanished. One moment she was there, a spectral figure on the ceiling, and the next, she was gone, as if she had never been there at all. I scanned the room, but there was no sign of her, no trace of her presence.

Confusion and disbelief swirled within me. What kind of person was she? What secrets did she hold? My mind raced with questions, each more baffling than the last. The logical part of me struggled to rationalize what I had seen, but deep down, I knew I had witnessed something beyond the realm of the ordinary.

The air in the bar felt heavier, charged with a strange energy. I felt a compelling urge to understand, to uncover the truth behind Braids and her otherworldly abilities. But for now, I was left in the dark, grappling with a reality that had suddenly become a lot more mysterious and unfathomable.

Chapter 12 - Shadows and Whispers

Braids

In those serene moments just after waking, when the world is still a blur and my surroundings are a mystery, there's a sense of contentment. Everything in my room looms in a tranquil, beautiful reality, free from judgment. It's a moment where reality and self are distinctly separated. But as the world gradually floats back into memory, I find myself yearning, if only briefly, for that ignorance again. To not know who I am or the meaning of the things that surround me, like the old books and trinkets on my shelves, bathed in the faded light seeping through silk curtains from the world outside.

Why do we endure it? Day after day, floating through existence without clear purpose. Today, I wandered the streets, my eyes falling on the unremarkable faces passing by. Men in hats and polished suits, their fingers adorned with rings, canes in hand. Women in flowing dresses, rippling in the November breeze. This town offers me so little.

Dressed in my usual black frilled skirt, button-down vest, white gloves, and frilled top hat, I prepared myself for the day. My belt, filled with various spices, clinked softly as I moved across the room to light the candelabra. The large, leather-bound spellbook on the table served as a haven for spiders, a testament to its age and disuse. The days have become routine, even with the minor disturbance caused by that man, Damian. It was still shocking to think that someone had come looking for the candelabra. But then again, it must have come from somewhere, and its previous owner must have known its specialness, even if they never delved into creating a spellbook fueled by curiosity like I did.

Feeling a sense of loneliness, I sought camaraderie from the only ones I could trust, the ones who listen but cannot act. I sprinkled cinnamon and tree bark bits into the candelabra's cylinders, watching as the small fire crackled to life. I placed a vine leaf, pulled from my neighbor's garden, over the fire. The leaf began to burn, emitting a popping green flame. I bathed my right hand in the green fire, watching as it glowed momentarily, green ash building under my fingertips. Then, with my other hand, I repeated the ritual with a crunchy dead leaf picked up from a previous walk. This time, the flame burned a rusty brown, and I carefully placed my left hand underneath, keeping the right behind my back to avoid cross-spell contamination.

Whispering an incantation, "Oh heavens, give me a kiss," I felt a sudden transformation. Black wings burst forth from my back, stretching high and wide in the dawning light of a new day. This ritual, part of my routine yet always magical, was a reminder of the extraordinary hidden within the ordinary. It was moments like these that kept the mundanity of life at bay, a small rebellion against the unremarkable existence that the town offered.

***

Walking home, my mind wandered through a maze of thoughts, reflecting on a lesson my father once shared.

"Trust," he said, "is giving someone the power to hurt you." This notion lingered in my head, weaving through my consciousness. Trust involves sharing a secret, something deeply personal, and in doing so, you hand over a piece of your vulnerability. That shared secret becomes a tool that could be used for emotional embarrassment or worse. We don't entrust others with information that we don't mind being spread; it's the secrets that matter, the ones that could wound us if revealed, that truly test our trust.

As I walked, the silhouettes of the buildings and trees around me faded into the background, mere shadows against the tapestry of my thoughts. In my world of magic and secrecy, trust becomes an even more complex concept. But then, there are the Gemool. They exist in a realm apart from mine, unable to influence anything or communicate with anyone in my reality. In their ethereal state, they are as removed from the consequences of the living world as one can be. I can confide in them, share my innermost thoughts without fear of repercussion, for they are inconsequential to the tangible reality.

In their passive existence, the Gemool are probably the closest to what one might consider trustworthy, even more so now than when they were alive. In life, they were passive, unassertive, and now, as mere echoes of their former selves, they wield even less influence.

These thoughts brought a sense of solace, a realization that in a world where trust is a rare commodity, I had found a safe haven in the company of spirits. They were my confidants, the keepers of my secrets, in a world where such a role was too risky for the living. As the city lights began to flicker on, casting a warm glow on the path ahead, I felt a sense of peace, knowing that in the midst of complexity and caution, I had found a simple, albeit unconventional, form of

trust.

Chapter 13 - Mysteries Unraveled

Damian:

Lying there beside Rosalie in the quiet aftermath of our intimacy, I found the stillness of the room unsettling. It was as if the walls themselves were privy to my inner turmoil, the secrets I kept buried. The subject of Braids, that enigmatic and elusive girl, inevitably wormed its way into our conversation.

"There's just something about her that gets under my skin," I said, the annoyance evident in my tone. I could feel my hands clenching unconsciously at the mere mention of her name.

Rosalie shifted slightly, her expression a blend of inquisitiveness and concern. Her eyes, always so perceptive, seemed to search mine for an unspoken truth. "She does seem quite the enigma," she mused, her voice tinged with a hint of fascination. "There's an air of mystery about her that's... intriguing."

I could feel the tension in the air thicken as we delved deeper into the topic. Rosalie's intuitive gaze never wavered, and her next question pierced right through my defenses. "Why are you so wrapped up in her affairs, Damian? What's really at stake here?"

Her inquiry hit me like a physical blow, unleashing a floodgate of pent-up emotions. I sat up abruptly, the bed sheets crumpling beneath me. "It's the candelabra she possesses," I blurted out, the words laced with a mix of anger and desperation. "I need it back, Rosalie. I just... It's important."

I rose from the bed and began pacing the room, each step echoing the chaos in my mind. The walls seemed to close in on me, making the room feel smaller, more confining. My thoughts were a whirlwind, centered on the candelabra and its mysterious connection to Braids. The more I dwelled on it, the more consumed I became by the need to reclaim it.

Rosalie watched me pace, her expression shifting from curiosity to concern. "Damian," she began, her voice a soothing balm to my frayed nerves. "You're letting this consume you. It's just an object."

But to me, it wasn't just an object. It was a symbol of something larger, a piece of a puzzle I was desperately trying to solve. And at the heart of that puzzle was Braids, a girl who defied explanation and who had unwittingly become the focal point of my obsession. As I continued to pace, the frustration and confusion swirling within me, I knew that I had to find a way to resolve this, to understand the connection between Braids, the candelabra, and the unsettling sense of destiny that hung over it all.

Seeking solace and clarity, I decided a carriage ride through the streets would do me good. The cool air and rhythmic clatter of horse hooves against the cobblestones always had a way of calming my restless thoughts. As I stepped outside, the sight of a black dog sitting just off the stoop caught my attention. It watched me intently with piercing, almost human-like eyes.

As I observed, the dog casually strolled into the dark alley next to my house. There, in the shadows, was Braids. The dog approached her and, in an almost surreal exchange, handed her a small bird bone. I watched, hidden by the corner of the building, as her hand glowed with an eerie orange hue upon touching the bone. It was as if she was momentarily granted a vision, seeing through the dog's eyes, witnessing my departure from the house. The scene was bizarre, like something out of a fantastical tale.

After a moment, Braids handed the bone back to the dog, which promptly scampered away, disappearing into the labyrinth of alleyways. I stood there for a moment longer, trying to make sense of what I had just witnessed. Shaking my head, I turned and made my way to the waiting carriage, the image of Braids and the dog etched in my mind.

Meanwhile, back in my bedroom, Rosalie's patience seemed to have worn thin. She sat by the window, her annoyance palpable. It was then that Braids, seizing the moment, worked her peculiar magic. Outside the window, a pale-headed rosella appeared, its vibrant plumage a stark contrast against the urban backdrop. The bird was not what it seemed, though; it was an insect transformed into a captivating bird.

Rosalie watched, mesmerized as the bird fluttered around the room. It was a beautiful, almost hypnotic display, capturing her full attention. Then, in a shocking turn, the bird burst into flames, vanishing as quickly as it had appeared. Rosalie, spurred by curiosity and concern, hastily dressed and rushed outside, eager to find the mysterious bird.

Unbeknownst to her, Braids was orchestrating these events, a master of manipulation and magic. Rosalie, completely unaware of the true nature of what she had witnessed, was now unwittingly caught in Braids' web of enchantment. As I rode through the streets, lost in my thoughts, I was oblivious to the intricate game Braids was playing, a game that was slowly entangling all of us in its complex weave.

***

Braids:

Disguised as an old man, I stood outside, watching as Rosalie emerged from the house, her eyes scanning the surroundings. The spell I had cast earlier, transforming an insect into a mesmerizing pale-headed rosella, had worked perfectly. Now, it was time to gauge its effect.

As Rosalie approached, her gaze still fixed on the sky where the bird had vanished, she seemed both bewildered and captivated. "Did you see a pretty bird?" she asked me, her voice tinged with a mix of wonder and confusion.

I nodded slowly, my voice altered to match my disguise. "Yes, a beautiful one. Flew right by here," I said, feigning the frailty of an old man. This was the perfect opportunity to learn more about Rosalie without revealing my true identity.

As our conversation continued, I subtly reached out and touched her shoulder, all the while casting a spell with my other hand, which remained hidden and cloaked in invisible flames. The spell was designed to turn the local animals against her subtly. It was a small nudge, but in the world of magic, even the slightest push could set a cascade of events into motion.

That night, as I lay in bed, I could feel the spell taking effect. Animals in the area, influenced by my enchantment, began to display unusual aggression towards Rosalie. Over the course of the week, the relentless harassment by the fauna grew. Birds squawked at her angrily, cats hissed in her presence, and dogs barked incessantly whenever she passed by. It was a gentle yet constant pressure, designed to unsettle and drive her away.

And it worked. Rosalie, unable to cope with the inexplicable hostility of the animals, decided to leave the city and return to France. The news of her departure reached me, and with it, a sense of satisfaction mixed with a twinge of regret. I had effectively removed her from the equation, but the act left a sour taste in my mouth.

Now, with Rosalie out of the way, I knew Damian's frustration would peak. He would be desperate to reclaim what he believed to be his, to put an end to my interference. But what he didn't realize was that this was no longer just a game of retrieval for him; it had become a personal vendetta for me as well. I had to be ready, for I knew he would come for the spellbook and me. The stakes had been raised, and I had to prepare for what was to come. This battle of wills and magic was about to escalate, and I needed to be one step ahead.

Chapter 14 - Enigmatic Alliances

Braids:

In the shop, amidst the clutter of antiquities and oddities, I was lost in my usual routine, dusting off relics that spoke more of the past than the present. The bell above the door jangled, heralding the entrance of a new customer. He was about my age, with an air of seriousness that seemed out of place in the whimsical disorder of the shop.

"Can I help you?" I asked, not bothering to mask my usual grumpiness.

"I'm Leon," he introduced himself, his tone straightforward. "I'm here about the candelabra. It belongs to my family. My brother, he's... well, he's quite upset about it."

I raised an eyebrow, my interest piqued despite myself. "Your brother sent you here to fetch a family heirloom? And he thinks I'm using it for magic? That's ridiculous," I scoffed, though internally, I was evaluating this Leon, trying to gauge his intentions.

Leon shifted uncomfortably. "He's convinced you have it. He doesn't understand why you'd want it so much. He's... not the easiest person to deal with."

I leaned against the counter, crossing my arms. "And why should I just hand it over to you? What makes your claim any more valid than mine?" I challenged, my tone tinged with skepticism.

To my surprise, Leon didn't react with anger or impatience. Instead, he listened, really listened, as I explained my side of the story. He didn't interrupt, didn't scoff, just took it all in with a calmness that was both unexpected and disarming.

"Well, at any rate, his girlfriend left town, and he's pretty upset about that too," Leon said after a moment, a hint of sympathy in his voice.

I couldn't help but smirk at the mention of the girlfriend. "I had nothing to do with that," I replied, though internally, I felt a sense of satisfaction at the chaos I had orchestrated.

Leon nodded, seemingly accepting my response. "I'll let him know I couldn't convince you. Thanks for your time," he said, turning to leave.

As he walked out, I found myself pondering over the encounter. I had expected Leon to be just another pawn of his brother, another antagonist in this tedious game. But his patience and willingness to hear me out left an impression. It was a rare thing to find someone who didn't immediately jump to conclusions or react with hostility.

I turned back to my work, the conversation with Leon replaying in my mind. It seemed the saga of the candelabra was far from over, but for now, I had an unexpected ally, or at the very least, someone who didn't view me as the villain in this twisted tale. The shop felt quieter after his departure, the dust settling back into its familiar patterns, and I, Braids, remained the keeper of secrets and spells, undeterred and unyielding.

***

Braids:

Alone on my rooftop, the cool night air wrapping around me, the weight of the day's revelations pressed heavily on my mind. The meeting with Leon had confirmed my worst suspicions: Damian knew about the candelabra and the magic I wielded. The thought of him being aware of my secrets filled me with a seething anger and a trace of fear.

In a fit of frustration, I let my emotions pour into my magic. My hands moved instinctively, channeling my fury into the plants in my rooftop garden. Vines twisted and writhed as if in agony, flowers wilted and blackened, leaves curled and dried up before my eyes. The destruction was a cathartic release, a physical manifestation of the turmoil within me.

But as the last petal fell, a pang of regret pierced through my anger. My garden, a haven of peace and solitude, lay ruined by my own hand. With a deep, steadying breath, I began the process of reversing the damage. My hands glowed with a soft green light as I whispered incantations of renewal and growth. Slowly, the plants responded, uncurling and reviving, their colors returning brighter and more vibrant than before.

This moment of breakdown and restoration on my rooftop was a stark reminder of the delicate balance I had to maintain. Damian's knowledge of the candelabra and my magic had changed everything. I couldn't afford to be reckless. The risks were too great now.

As I stood among my rejuvenated plants, a resolution formed within me. I needed to lay low, to curtail my use of magic. I had to throw Damian off, make him believe that his suspicions were unfounded. For a while, at least, I would have to act normal, blend in, and hide the extraordinary beneath a facade of the mundane.

The rooftop, bathed in moonlight, felt like a crossroads. The path ahead was fraught with uncertainty, but I was determined to navigate it with caution and cunning. I would protect my secrets, my magic, at all costs. The night air grew colder, whispering secrets of its own, and I, Braids, stood resolute, a shadowy figure in a world where magic and reality intertwined in a dangerous dance.

Chapter 15 - Cautious Engagements

Braids:

Days passed in a monotonous blur, each one blending into the next with an unremarkable sameness. Without the use of magic, my world felt constricted, like a beautiful, dark bird caged and unable to spread its wings. The frustration of hiding my true nature gnawed at me, a constant reminder of the precarious situation I found myself in. The shop, once a sanctuary of secrets and spells, now felt like a prison, its walls echoing the silence of my subdued powers.

Just as I was brooding over my constrained existence, a knock at the door jolted me from my reverie. Standing there, to my surprise, was Leon. His presence was as unexpected as it was unwelcome. "Braids, I was wondering if you'd like to go out with me," he said, a hint of earnestness in his voice. "I know my brother doesn't like you, but I do."

I stared at him, incredulous. "What the hell?" was my first thought. Trust was not a commodity I dealt in freely, and Leon's sudden interest seemed suspicious at best. Was this another ploy by his brother? A way to gather information or catch me off-guard?

Despite my skepticism, a plan began to form in my mind. If I kept my magic hidden and my lips sealed, Leon wouldn't be able to glean anything of value. And perhaps, just perhaps, I could use this as an opportunity to learn more about him and his brother. It was a risky game, but one that could potentially yield useful information.

"Alright," I said, feigning a casual interest. "Let's go out."

As we walked through the streets, I kept my guard up, carefully choosing my words and actions. Leon, for his part, seemed genuinely interested, but I couldn't shake off the feeling that there was more to this than met the eye. I watched him, analyzing his every word and gesture, looking for any hint of duplicity.

The evening passed in a blur of cautious conversation and veiled glances. Leon was an enigma, and I found myself reluctantly intrigued by his company. Yet, the shadow of his brother loomed over us, a silent specter in our midst.

Returning to the shop later that night, I felt a mix of relief and frustration. The outing had yielded little in the way of useful information, but it had confirmed one thing: Leon was not to be underestimated. As I locked the shop door behind me, the familiar sense of solitude enveloped me once more. In this world of shadows and secrets, trust was a rare and dangerous thing, and I was more determined than ever to guard mine fiercely.

Chapter 16 - Echoes of Dreams

Braids:

The evening with Leon unfolded under the soft glow of fireflies, their tiny lights flickering like stars fallen to earth. We sat sipping tea by the firelight, the warmth chasing away the evening chill. Despite the picturesque setting, I couldn't shake off the feeling of unease, the sense of playing a part in a script I hadn't read.

"No, Braids is not my given name," I found myself saying in response to his inquiry, my voice tinged with a hint of nostalgia. "But it's what everyone calls me. It started as a nickname in childhood, owing to my hair always being in two long braids. And now, at 22, here I am, living above my father's pawn shop in a town that feels both familiar and foreign."

Our conversation meandered through trivialities. "How are you?" he asked, the usual politeness in his tone.

"I'm fine, thanks," I replied automatically, though the truth was more complicated. My mind drifted to a response I had never dared to give: "Well, you know, the bees are really starting to get to me – they get tangled in my hair a lot when I sleep on the grass. Buzz."

The evening took an unexpected turn when Leon abruptly stopped and confronted a man who had been trailing us discreetly. It turned out to be a private investigator hired by his brother. Leon's anger was palpable, his frustration with his brother's actions clear. This revelation made me pause – was Leon genuinely not part of his brother's schemes?

Later that night, as I lay in bed, my thoughts were a whirlwind of confusion and symbolism. Vivid images danced in my mind's eye. I imagined myself soaring over the city, black wings carrying me to the countryside, over lush greenery and grand trees, until I reached a serene blue lagoon.

Landing gently by the water's edge, my reflection in the lagoon was nothing but a shadow, the water's depths revealing only a ghostly image. A majestic oryx appeared on the opposite bank, its long, twisting horns and striking throat flap demanding my attention. The animal bent to drink, its movements graceful yet powerful.

The scene shifted from morning to dusk in an instant, casting a golden hue over the lagoon. I watched the oryx drink, its horns bobbing, tail twitching. The symbolism of the oryx – a creature of hope and resilience – was not lost on me, yet its meaning in my dream remained a mystery.

As I drifted off to sleep, the image of the oryx stayed with me, a symbol of something significant yet elusive. In the complexity of my life, where trust was a rare commodity and every encounter a potential game of deception, the oryx stood as a beacon of something purer, a reminder that amidst the shadows and intrigue, there was still room for hope.

Chapter 17 - Unveiled Secrets

Damian:

Under the cloak of dusk, I found myself in an obscure alleyway, the address on the slip of paper in my hand my only guide. "Mr. Ambrose Dravenwood; 42 Ashhollow Lane." The faded sign creaked gently in the evening breeze, confirming I was at the right location. With a deep breath, I mustered a knock on the door. No response. I knocked again, harder this time, and heard the faint sound of movement inside – chairs scraping, footsteps approaching.

The door creaked open, revealing a tall, thin man with unkempt brown hair peeking out from under a grey hat. His piercing dark green eyes scanned me rapidly, flickering from my face to my hands and then darting around, taking in every detail of my appearance and surroundings.

"Hello, Mr. Dravenwood?" I inquired, trying to mask my impatience.

He scrutinized me with a calculating gaze, his eyes darting from my hands to my shoes and then off into the alleyway, as if seeing more than just the physical form before him. "Who are you? And what do you want?" His voice was as sharp as his gaze.

Introducing myself as Damian, I explained my need for his investigative services. He scrutinized me further, his eyes reflecting the torchlight like a cat's as they scanned me from head to toe. Finally, he invited me inside, sealing the door behind us with an array of locks.

"So, you demand my services. How did you hear about me?" he questioned.

I explained my connections, hoping to impress upon him the seriousness of my request. "I need you to delve into the life of a particular girl," I said, my voice steady despite the gravity of what I was about to entrust to this stranger.

Dravenwood's brow furrowed in skepticism as I detailed my request – the theft of a family heirloom, a candelabra, and a large handwritten book, both of which I believed were in the possession of a girl whose father owned a pawn shop in Edinburgh.

"A candelabra, you say?" Dravenwood questioned, his tone a mix of curiosity and disbelief.

"Yes, and a book," I added quickly. "But you must not open it. It's personal."

Dravenwood leaned back in his chair, the shadows playing across his face. He warned me of the cost of such a venture, but I was resolute. The secrecy, the clean execution, and the discovery of their hiding place were paramount.

"I will do it," he finally agreed after I assured him of my honesty and the nature of what we were dealing with. "Witches," I had said, the word hanging in the air between us.

We shook hands, the deal sealed. I paid him a third of the fee upfront, the rest to be delivered with each item.

Days later, Dravenwood returned, successful in his mission. He handed me the candelabra and the book. I was astounded at the depth of knowledge within the pages, far surpassing what my great-grandmother had ever achieved. My next step was clear – I needed to visit my grandmother in another city for further insight.

As Dravenwood prepared to leave, he offered one last piece of information, something he had gleaned from his time in the girl's room. "You know, there is power in knowing a witch's name," he said, his voice low. "I'll tell you what it is for an extra shilling."

I regarded him warily, then flicked him a silver coin. He leaned in close and whispered, "Adella Niamh Kaitlin-Hayes." Then, without another word, he turned and disappeared into the night.

Quickly, I scribbled the name on a scrap of paper and tucked it safely into my suit pocket. This was a significant development – a name held power, especially in the world of witchcraft. With this new knowledge and the stolen items in my possession, I felt a step closer to unraveling the mysteries that had entangled me. The game had changed, and I was now a player with a hand to play.

Chapter 18 - Clashing Perspectives

Damian:

The tension in the room was palpable as Leon burst in, his eyes blazing with a mix of accusation and disbelief. He slammed the door shut behind him, the sound echoing through the space like a gunshot.

"Damian, what the hell was that about?" Leon's voice was sharp, cutting through the air. "Why were you having me followed on my date with Braids?"

I looked at him, my own frustration simmering just below the surface. "It wasn't about you, Leon," I snapped back. "This has nothing to do with you. It's her – Braids. She's a witch, and I have proof!"

Leon's expression shifted from anger to confusion. "A witch? Really, Damian? This is what this is about? You're obsessed!"

I could feel my anger boiling over. "Obsessed? No, I'm not obsessed. I'm trying to protect what's mine. She took something from me, something important. And she chased away Rosalie. She manipulated everything!"

Leon shook his head, disbelief written all over his face. "You're fixated, Damian. This isn't about some family heirloom or your ex-girlfriend. This is about you not being able to let go of something that's clearly not yours anymore."

The argument escalated, our voices rising with each accusation and denial. "You don't understand, Leon. You don't know what she's capable of, the things I've seen. She's dangerous."

"Dangerous? Or just someone who doesn't fit into your neat little world?" Leon countered, his tone laced with frustration.

We were at an impasse, two men driven by our own perceptions and motives, unable to see eye to eye. The room felt smaller, the air between us charged with the electricity of our confrontation.

As Leon turned to leave, his parting words hung in the air. "You need to take a good look at yourself, Damian. Figure out what you're really fighting for."

Left alone in the room, I felt a mix of anger and helplessness. Leon didn't understand; he couldn't see the truth as I did. But his words gnawed at me, a nagging doubt in the back of my mind. Was I really doing the right thing? Was my pursuit of Braids driven by a need for justice, or was it something darker, something more personal?

The evening left me unsettled, the echoes of our argument reverberating in my thoughts. I knew one thing for certain – my quest was far from over. I needed to uncover the truth about Braids, to expose her for what she truly was. But as I sat there, alone with my thoughts, I couldn't shake off the feeling that this journey was leading me down a path I hadn't anticipated, one that might change everything I thought I knew.

Chapter 19 - Ethereal Reflections

Braids:

The Gemool, my ghostly companions, gathered around their ethereal poker table, their cards fluttering in the ghostly breeze. The air in the room felt dense, heavy with the weight of unspoken thoughts and centuries-old wisdom. I had sought their counsel following my date with Leon, my mind a tumult of emotions and fears.

One of the Gemool, his transparent form flickering like a candle in the wind, spoke up, his voice a hollow echo of a life long past. "The nature of mankind is suffering," he began, his eyes, or where his eyes would have been, fixed on me. "Many of us try to live without causing harm, without offending, unless provoked... and yet, we fail. It is inevitable that we cause damage to others simply by existing. Our desires often conflict, and in fulfilling our own, we may inadvertently harm another."

I listened, the words resonating within the depths of my being. "But what if I choose to isolate myself, to build walls around me to protect others from the pain I might cause, and to shield myself from their rejection?" I asked, my voice barely above a whisper.

His response came as a sigh, a sound that seemed to carry the weight of ages. "One cannot live in a bubble, no matter how hard one tries. We must navigate life, stepping carefully, but understanding that we are not wholly responsible for the feelings of others. They are shaped by their own experiences and reactions. When we act without malice, we must not be too harsh on ourselves when things go awry and others are hurt."

Another Gemool chimed in, his voice a rustling like dry leaves. "And even in your isolation, you cannot escape the gaze of the world. A passing stranger may see you, form an opinion, perhaps even fall in love. Without intending, without associating, you have influenced another's heart. To avoid interaction entirely is to cause its own form of heartbreak."

Their words hung in the air, a tapestry of truth and sorrow. I stood there, amidst my spectral friends, realizing the complexity of my situation. My desire to protect Leon and myself was noble, but perhaps it was also futile. In this world of shadows and light, interaction and influence were inevitable.

I looked around at the Gemool, their ghostly forms a reminder of lives once lived, of choices made and paths taken. In their silent company, I found a strange comfort. They were my confidants in a world where trust was a rare gem, hidden in the dark mines of human interaction. As I left them to their eternal game of poker, their words echoed in my mind, a reminder that life, in all its complexity, was a dance of shadows and light, of connections made and broken, of hearts touched and sometimes, inadvertently, wounded.

***

That brisk evening, as I made my way home, the sky was a tapestry of overcast grey, reminiscent of a gothic painting. Clouds, like layers of grey wool, churned and tumbled over one another in a restless dance. I closed my eyes for a moment, feeling the dense weight of my thoughts, as if my mind were filled with thick fog.

Stretching my back, I found a semblance of comfort in the cold air, my gaze lifting to the endless grey abyss above. Pulling my black fleece jacket tighter around me, I wrapped my arms around myself, seeking warmth in the chill of the evening.

As I walked, the faces of passersby seemed to blend into the monochrome landscape of the city. To my eyes, the world was predominantly grey, devoid of vibrancy, save for certain exceptions. My spells, the creations of my magic, stood out in stark contrast, vibrant and full of life against the dreary backdrop. They were like bold strokes of oil paint on a canvas of grey, a vivid representation of the Gemool's apt analogy.

Even in this muted world, some natural elements retained their own colors. Wild animals - birds, feral cats, and the occasional deer that dared to wander into the central city gardens - all moved with an inherent vibrancy. The plants there too were alive with color, their greenery lush and thriving amidst the urban sprawl.

My thoughts drifted to my spectral companions, the Gemool. In death, they had come to understand the beauty of life, yet they were forever barred from truly experiencing it. Their existence, confined to the shadows of a bar, was a poignant reminder of the fleeting nature of existence.

But in my unique position, I could tap into their world, draw wisdom from their ethereal existence. Why them, these forlorn spirits? Perhaps it was a reflection of my own inner need for safety, a desire to be sheltered among those who could not harm me. There was an ironic warmth in their company, a sense of belonging amidst the departed.

As I continued my walk, my father's words about trust echoed in my mind. To trust was to give someone the power to hurt you, to expose a part of yourself to potential pain. The Gemool, in their spectral state, were perhaps the only beings I could truly trust. They were removed from the tangible world, unable to influence or betray.

Lost in these thoughts, I approached the pawn shop, my place of work and refuge. As I neared the entrance, my wings, which had carried me through the night, began to dissolve into the air, their violet hues fading like leaves carried away by an autumn wind. They were my escape, my freedom, but here, in the realm of the living, they had no place. With a final glance at the sky, I stepped into the shop, ready to resume my role in the waking world.

Chapter 20 - The Chase Intensifies

Braids:

After another day's work in the pawn shop, I made my way to the rooftop, my personal sanctuary above the cluttered world below. The garden on the roof, my little haven amidst the urban sprawl, was a stark contrast to the shop's cramped quarters filled with the relics of other people's lives.

I stretched out on my back, the cool, uneven surface of the rooftop a welcome reprieve. Above me, the sky was a canvas of shifting clouds, painted in hues of white and grey against the azure backdrop. The sun peeked through occasionally, casting fleeting shadows that danced across my face. A soft breeze whisked across the rooftop, teasing bits of my bangs into the air, making them flutter like whimsical string kites.

As I lay there, a sigh escaped my lips, a sound of contentment mixed with a lingering sense of longing. Something felt incomplete, a piece of the picture that was missing. My gaze shifted to the side, where my top hat lay abandoned on the roof tiles. With a fluid motion, I reached over, the fabric feeling familiar and comforting under my fingertips. I placed it carefully upon my head, adjusting it with a practiced ease. My bangs settled back onto my forehead, framing my face with a sense of completion.

Sitting up, I took a moment to take in the view. The rooftop garden was alive with the vibrant colors of flowers and plants, a stark contrast to the grey cityscape surrounding it. It was a world of my own making, a blend of nature and magic, where I could escape the mundane reality below.

The rooftop was more than just a physical space; it was a reflection of my inner self, a place where I could be truly me, away from prying eyes and the weight of expectations. Here, among the whispering leaves and the scent of blooming flowers, I found a peace that was rare in my life. It was a place where I could dream, plan, and simply exist without the need to hide or pretend.

As the wind continued to play with my hair, I closed my eyes and let the tranquility of the garden wash over me. In this moment, on this rooftop, I was free – free from the burdens of my secrets, free from the complexities of a life intertwined with magic and mystery.

Descending from my rooftop refuge, I retreated to my room, a sense of weariness enveloping me. The stone ceiling above seemed to loom, a silent witness to my inner turmoil. I collapsed onto my bed, the mattress barely cushioning the weight of my exhaustion. For a moment, I just lay there, staring blankly at the ceiling, a deep sigh escaping my lips.

After some time, I mustered the energy to rise. My body felt stiff, every movement accompanied by the crack of joints and the stretch of unused muscles. I gravitated towards my desk, where my organized collection of spices waited, their scents a reminder of the magic they held. I scooped some ground cinnamon into the fire, watching as a spark of yellow-orange danced and flickered from the flames.

Turning to consult my bookshelf for further insight into cinnamon's properties, I froze. The shelf where my spellbook usually rested was glaringly empty. A sense of panic gripped me as I frantically searched the room – under the bed, among the scattered papers on my desk – but it was nowhere to be found. The realization hit me like a physical blow: could Damian have broken in and stolen it?

A rush of horror swept through me, my heart pounding furiously, a hummingbird trapped in a cage of ribs. My head throbbed with a sharp pain, each beat echoing the betrayal I felt. I had let my guard down, allowed myself to feel something other than disdain for Damian, and now I was paying the price.

I sank to my knees, the cold stone floor a stark contrast to the warmth of my tears. My black wings, usually a symbol of strength and freedom, now felt like a suffocating shroud, enveloping me in a cocoon of despair. I curled into myself, overwhelmed by a sense of defeat and betrayal.

The laughter of the Gemool, those ghostly companions who had warned me of the dangers of trust, echoed in my memory. I should have known better, should have been more vigilant. In my moment of weakness, I had exposed myself to this heartache, this loss.

Lying there, wrapped in the dark embrace of my wings, I felt like a failure. My soul felt crushed, my spirit broken. The world seemed to spin around me, a chaotic whirlwind of emotions and regrets. I had been bested, and the price was the loss of a part of me, a part I had cherished and nurtured. The weight of this realization pressed down on me, a burden too heavy to bear in that vulnerable moment.

As I lay on the ground, engulfed in my own sorrow and self-loathing, a transformation began within me. The despair that had momentarily weakened me soon gave way to a fiery anger. This shift in emotion was like a spark igniting a dormant volcano, and I could feel my power returning, fueled by rage. I pushed myself onto my knees, a renewed sense of determination coursing through me.

Standing up, I approached the candelabra, my hands trembling with a mixture of fury and anticipation. I rummaged through my drawer, my mind racing back to some of the more sinister spells I had mastered. As I recalled them, my hands burst into unnatural red flames, a physical manifestation of the anger burning within.

Around me, the air crackled with dark energy. A spectral skull appeared, screeching as it orbited my head, its jaw snapping open and closed in a macabre dance. From my black wings sprouted razor-sharp bony blades at the joints, turning them into lethal weapons. Demonic horns, curved like a scythe's blade, emerged from my forehead, symbolizing the rage that had taken hold of me.

A new pair of ears, large and fox-like with striped patterns, sprouted from the sides of my head. They provided me with supernatural hearing abilities, allowing me to pick up even the faintest of sounds. I could rotate them at will, focusing on distant noises with the precision of a predator.

Refilling my spell belt with various ingredients, I prepared for what was to come. A tiny green flame appeared at the base of my wrist, acting like a portal through which I could recast my spells. I burned some thyme in it, and with a snap of my fingers, I teleported onto the rooftop.

There, under the night sky, I spread my black wings wide, an embodiment of the fearsome hunter I had become. My fox ears adjusted to the sounds of the city below, fine-tuning my senses to the world around me. With a determined look, I ran to the edge of the roof and leaped into the air.

As I took flight, my form was that of a demonic creature, a sight to behold had the people below been able to witness it. The moonlight glinted off my razor-sharp wing blades, casting eerie shadows as I soared through the night. I was a force to be reckoned with, a being of power and vengeance, ready to reclaim what was mine and confront those who had wronged me.

As I landed heavily on the front steps of Damian's residence, my mind was a tempest of fury and determination. I was fully prepared to tear the door down if necessary. My eyes, still burning with a vengeful fire, focused intently on the entrance. I rapped sharply on the door, ready to confront Damian, to catch him unawares and demand the return of what he had stolen from me.

The sound of footsteps approached from within, and I braced myself for the confrontation. I was teetering on the edge, my thoughts oscillating between a controlled accusation and an unleashed inferno of rage.

However, the face that greeted me was not Damian's. A wave of confusion momentarily washed over me.

"Hi, can I help you?" The man at the door was unfamiliar, his tone polite yet cautious.

"Is Damian here?" I managed to say, my voice strained, teeth gritted in an effort to restrain my anger.

"Oh, he has just gone away on recent business, and I'm afraid you just missed him. I'm his brother, Leon, by the way. Nice to meet you!" Leon's introduction was friendly, but it did nothing to quell the storm brewing inside me.

A low growl escaped my throat as I bowed my head slightly, turning to leave. I could feel the cold stone of the stoop under my hand as I descended, each step fueling my resolve. Damian had fled, confirming my worst fears – he really had stolen the candelabra and my book.

"I didn't get your name?" Leon called after me, his voice echoing in the quiet street.

Without turning back, I kept walking, my black wings folding tightly against my back. "Tell him Braids was here," I called over my shoulder, my voice laced with a cold edge. He would know who had come looking for him.

As I walked away, my mind was already racing ahead, plotting my next move. Damian had fled to the train station, no doubt to escape the city. The realization that he had indeed taken what was mine fueled my anger further, turning it into a burning resolve. I would track him down, no matter where he tried to hide. This was more than just a theft; it was a betrayal, a challenge to the very core of who I was. And I, Braids, would not let this go unanswered.

As I turned the corner into the alley, the cool dampness of the air mingled with the scent of rain on cobblestone. Leon did not pursue me; I heard the door close behind him as I gazed up at the overcast sky, thick with clouds that promised more rain.

With a pinch of cinnamon in my left hand, I called forth a green flame, a beacon in the dim light of the alley. It was time to enlist the aid of the city's other inhabitants - the ravens and stray dogs that roamed the streets. "Go scout for me," I whispered, my voice barely more than a breath, yet carrying the weight of my command.

The ravens ascended into the grey sky, their black silhouettes stark against the clouds, while the dogs bolted off, their paws thudding against the stone. I cast a spell of dark vision, rubbing my pointer finger from my flame-lit hand over my eyes, granting me the ability to see through their eyes, to share their keen senses.

The world as seen through the animals was a tapestry of smells and sounds, a cacophony of the city's hidden life. They knew Damian's scent, and they were soon on his trail, their instincts guiding them unerringly. But the signs all pointed to one conclusion – Damian was not in town. He had fled, just as I had suspected.

A dog and a raven converged at the train station. Through their eyes, I saw the dog circle the tracks, sniffing intently. It stopped, confirming my worst fears - Damian had been there but was now long gone. The raven perched on the platform, its gaze following the tracks that stretched away from the city, leading to unknown destinations.

The connection was abruptly broken as a train pulled into the station, startling the dog. It yelped, the spell dissipating, and my vision snapped back to my own. The dog, no longer under the spell's influence, abandoned its task, overwhelmed by the noise and movement around it.

Left alone in the alley, my connection to the animals severed, I felt a surge of frustration. Damian had slipped through my grasp, vanished like a ghost in the night. But I wasn't one to give up so easily. My resolve hardened; this was a setback, but not the end. Damian may have evaded me for now, but I would find him. No matter where he ran, no matter where he hid, I would track him down and reclaim what was mine. My journey was far from over, and I, Braids, was not one to be underestimated.

Chapter 21 - Threshold of Revelations

Braids:

Determination coursed through my veins as I unfurled my black wings, their span casting a shadow on the cobblestones of the alley. I was a creature of the night, a blend of darkness and purpose. With a leap, I took to the air, soaring above the city, my destination set southward.

But first, I needed a clue, a lead to where Damian could have fled. I swooped down to the train station, blending into the shadows as I perused the departure times and locations.

Among the hustle and bustle of travelers, I was a specter, unnoticed and silent. The station's clock ticked away the seconds, a constant reminder of the urgency of my quest.

There, on the schedule, I found my answer. A train had departed just five minutes ago, another ten. My window of opportunity was narrowing, but not yet closed. I could still catch him.

With a renewed sense of purpose, I launched myself into the sky once more, my wings cutting through the air. I followed the tracks, the steel ribbons that stretched into the countryside, a path that I hoped would lead me to Damian.

The landscape below changed as I flew, the city's dense buildings giving way to open fields and patches of forest. The countryside was a tapestry of greens and browns, peaceful and undisturbed, a stark contrast to the turmoil within me.

As I flew, I spotted a house in the distance, nestled amidst the rolling hills. It was secluded, a solitary structure that seemed to hold secrets within its walls. A hunch told me this was where I would find Damian.

I descended, landing gracefully near the house. It was a quaint, countryside abode, but something about it felt off, as if it were hiding more than it showed. I approached cautiously, my senses heightened, alert to any sign of danger.

To my surprise, I was not alone. Leon, Damian's brother, was there, his presence unexpected yet not entirely unwelcome. There was a tension in the air, an unspoken understanding that we were both here for the same reason – Damian.

"Leon," I called out, my voice steady despite the whirlwind of emotions inside me. "What are you doing here?"

Leon turned to face me, his expression a mix of surprise and wariness. "Braids," he said, a hint of recognition in his voice. "I could ask you the same question."

The air between Leon and me crackled with an unspoken tension, an electric charge that seemed to hum with the secrets and lies that had led us to this moment. We stood there, outside the quaint yet oddly foreboding country house, each of us driven by our own motives yet bound by a common thread - Damian.

Leon's presence was a curious element in this intricate tapestry Damian had woven. His eyes held a wariness, a guarded caution that mirrored my own. "Why are you here, Braids? What do you want with my brother?" Leon's voice held a mixture of suspicion and a plea for understanding.

I weighed my words carefully, my mind racing with the myriad of emotions that Damian's betrayal had stirred within me. "I'm here for what he took from me," I responded, my voice steady yet laced with an undercurrent of anger. "Damian stole something precious, something that's more than just an object. It's a part of who I am."

Leon's gaze flickered, a shadow of doubt crossing his features. It was clear he was torn, caught between familial loyalty and the growing realization that his brother's actions were far from innocent.

"We need to find him, Leon. Your brother has entangled us both in his web of deception. It's time we faced him and demanded answers." My words were a call to action, an appeal to the part of Leon that sought the truth as much as I did.

Reluctantly, Leon nodded, his resolve hardening. "Let's do it then. Let's find out what Damian's been hiding."

Together, we approached the house, the building seeming to loom larger with each step. The countryside around us was eerily silent, the usual sounds of nature subdued, as if the land itself was holding its breath, awaiting the unfolding drama.

As we reached the door, I felt a surge of adrenaline, a mix of fear and anticipation. What lay beyond that threshold? What secrets did Damian harbor within these walls? The answers were close now, almost within reach.

With a determined push, we opened the door and stepped inside. The house was quiet, the air still, as if it were hiding its secrets, protecting its owner's misdeeds. But I was undeterred. Whatever Damian was hiding, whatever truths lay buried here, I was ready to uncover them. The game was reaching its climax, and I, Braids, was ready to confront whatever lay ahead.

Chapter 22 - Altered Paths

Braids:

Fury coursed through my veins like a tempest, driving me forward with a singular purpose. Damian had taken what was mine – the candelabra, the source of my power, and my precious spellbook. The betrayal cut deep, igniting a fire within me that could not be quenched.

With my black angel wings unfurled, I soared above the moving train, a dark figure against the twilight sky. The wind howled around me, echoing my rage as I scanned each carriage, searching for Damian. He was fleeing to another city, seeking to uncover secrets from our family's past with the candelabra. But I would not let him escape so easily.

I leapt into the air, allowing the train to pass beneath me before landing again with a thud on the roof. My eyes, burning with a fierce green light, were enhanced with a special spell that allowed me to see through the carriage ceilings. I peered down, searching intently for any sign of Damian.

There he was – sitting inside, unaware of the storm that was about to descend upon him. I quickly prepared a new spell, one that would allow me to slip through the solid roof and confront him directly. Muttering the incantation, I felt the fabric of reality warp around me, and in a blink, I passed through the roof, landing gracefully on the carriage floor.

My wings spread wide upon landing, an imposing sight that drew gasps from the other passengers. I stood up, my gaze fixed on Damian, who looked back at me with a defiance that matched my own anger.

Without a word, I extended my arms, channeling my fury into a spell directed at the carriage windows. The glass trembled, then gathered into a swirling orb before shattering into a thousand shards. With a flick of my wrist, I directed the shards towards Damian, a deadly storm of glass propelled by my wrath.

Damian reacted quickly, conjuring a protective barrier, but the ferocity of my attack was relentless. Glass clinked harmlessly off his shield, falling like rain around us. Our eyes locked in a battle of wills, anger meeting anger, power clashing with power.

The air in the carriage crackled with magical energy, a tangible manifestation of our confrontation. I was a tempest, a force of nature unleashed, and Damian, though standing his ground, was now facing the full extent of my fury.

"This ends now, Damian," I hissed, my voice low and dangerous. "You've taken what's mine, and for that, you will pay."

The tension between us was like a live wire, sparking and hissing in the confined space of the carriage. This was more than just a battle over a stolen item; it was a clash of blood, of legacy, of betrayal. And I, Braids, with my wings of darkness and eyes aflame, was ready to reclaim what was rightfully mine.

As I stood there, wings outstretched and fury in my eyes, ready to unleash further spells upon Damian, he did something unexpected. With a calm, almost calculated tone, he uttered a name – my full name, one I had kept hidden from the world. "Adella Niamh Kaitlin-Hayes."

The effect was immediate and devastating. The power coursing through me, fueling my spells and my wrath, dissipated like mist under the sun. I felt my magical defenses crumbling, each spell I had cast unraveling. My wings, once a symbol of strength and freedom, now felt heavy and useless. I stood there, feeling utterly vulnerable and exposed, the shock of betrayal etching itself onto my face.

Damian continued, his voice laced with a cold authority. "Now, you might as well just sit down and behave until the next stop on this train. Then you leave, or I call the authorities for your sneaking on without a ticket. They are also ready to strike in case you want to harass me further. Now, please, leave me in peace with what is rightfully mine. I am sorry it had to come to this, but I knew you had my grandmother's spells from the beginning."

His words were like a slap, a harsh reminder of my newfound helplessness. I was hotheaded and angry, but utterly powerless. My spells, my magical prowess, all had been stripped away with the mere utterance of my true name.

"How though... Where did you learn my name?!... And my candelabra," I managed to stammer, my voice a mix of disbelief and anger.

"Now please, Adella, don't make a scene," Damian said, his use of my first name adding insult to injury.

I felt a burning humiliation, mixed with an overwhelming sense of defeat. Damian had outmaneuvered me, taken away my most potent weapon – my magic. I was left with nothing but my raw emotions, a storm of anger and frustration with no outlet.

As the train continued its journey, the rhythmic clacking of the wheels on the tracks was a stark contrast to the chaos of emotions raging within me. I had been bested, my power nullified by the one person I had least expected to wield such knowledge against me.

In that moment, on that train, I was no longer Braids, the fearsome wielder of magic. I was Adella, stripped of my defenses, forced to confront the reality of my situation. Damian had the upper hand, and I was at his mercy, a position I had never imagined I would find myself in. The journey ahead loomed uncertain, and for the first time in a long while, I felt truly lost.

Sitting side by side in that train carriage, a heavy silence engulfed us. I could feel the tears pricking at the corners of my eyes, a torrent of emotions threatening to overflow. I was beaten, reduced to a state of vulnerability I hadn't experienced since I was a child. Memories, long buried, began to resurface – moments of helplessness and despair.

A specific memory flashed before my eyes: the day my mother died. I had tried everything in my power, every spell and incantation I knew, to save her. But it was all in vain. My magic, which I had believed to be my strength, had failed me when I needed it most. I remembered crying then, a deep, wrenching sorrow that had seemed to consume me. I had blamed myself, thinking if only I had been stronger, better, more skilled in my craft...

But now, sitting here, defeated yet again, I refused to let those tears fall, especially not in front of Damian. I had grown since those days, become stronger and more resilient. I would not show him my weakness, not give him the satisfaction of seeing me break down.

After a time, I found my voice again, a whisper of defiance in the silence. "You know, I've had that candelabra nearly my whole life, since I was a young girl. I got it in my pawn shop. By now, it was rightfully mine, more than yours. Your family legitimately forfeited it. Think about the morals in that."

My words hung in the air, a challenge to Damian's claim of ownership. The candelabra had been a part of my life for so long, it had become a piece of my identity. To have it taken away so abruptly, so unjustly, was a blow that went deeper than the loss of mere property. It was a theft of a part of myself, a violation of the life I had built.

Damian remained silent, his expression unreadable. Whether my words had any effect on him, I couldn't tell. But in that moment, I realized that this was about more than just the candelabra or the spellbook. It was about my right to my own life, my own choices. I had grown up with that candelabra, learned from it, and become who I was because of it. And no one, not even Damian, had the right to take that away from me.

Damian's words were a cold dismissal, a final twist of the knife he had already driven deep. "Are you really more deserving, to take what is no longer yours?" he mused, his gaze fixed ahead, as if contemplating some distant thought. "It is a family treasure, not meant for outsiders. It was wrongfully and mistakenly sold. Though, I must say, I am impressed by you, Braids. You have taken it to an amazing level and really lived it with heart. Devotion and strong will like that which you possess can be put to very productive places. Good luck in your future endeavors. I believe this is your stop coming up..."

His words were like a hollow echo in my ears, a blend of grudging admiration and finality. As the train slowed to a halt at the station, Damian stood up, and I followed suit, still in a daze. He escorted me to the door, his actions formal, almost courteous, in stark contrast to the harsh reality of what he had done.

Stepping off the train, I found myself in a state of shock, a passivity that was foreign to me. It was as if Damian's utterance of my full name had not only stripped me of my powers but also part of my essence, my very being.

As the train began to move again, Damian leaned out of the window, calling back to me, "Don't worry, the passivity will wear off soon. But after this point, you don't have to feel that again, as you can no longer be a witch without a source, the candelabra. Your name is back to ordinary once you are cut off from it."

His words were a final blow, the closing of a chapter in my life that I had never anticipated ending. The train pulled away, carrying with it the candelabra, my spellbook, and a part of my identity. I stood there, motionless, on the platform, my mind struggling to process the enormity of what had just happened.

I was no longer Braids, the witch with the power to bend reality to my will. I was just Adella now, ordinary and powerless. The realization was overwhelming, a void where my magic and purpose used to be.

As the last car of the train disappeared from view, the full weight of my loss settled upon me. I was alone, bereft of the powers that had defined me for so long. The future, once a canvas of endless possibilities, now seemed bleak and uncertain.

But even in that moment of despair, a spark of my old self flickered within me. Damian had taken my powers, but he couldn't take away who I was at my core – resilient, determined, and unbroken. I might have lost my magic, but I still had my will, and I would find a way to move forward, to rebuild and redefine myself. This was not the end of my story, just a new, unexpected chapter.

Chapter 23 - Rediscovery in Silence

Braids:

Days turned into a blur, each one indistinguishable from the last. The loss of my powers, the candelabra, and my spellbook had left me adrift, like a ship without a sail in a vast, empty ocean. I wandered the city aimlessly, my heart heavy with a grief I couldn't shake off. The park became my refuge, a place where I could be alone with my thoughts, away from the reminders of the life I had lost.

I found myself sitting on a bench, staring blankly at the autumn leaves that danced in the wind. The vibrant colors of nature, once a source of inspiration for my spells, now seemed to mock my powerlessness. "How will I get it back?"

I whispered to myself, my voice barely audible. The question hung in the air, unanswered and heavy. "Can I live without being a witch? It's all I have…"

Being a witch had been my identity, my purpose. It was the lens through which I had viewed the world, the means by which I had interacted with it. Now, stripped of that part of myself, I felt lost, unsure of who I was without my magic.

The bench outside Damian's place became my vigil. I sat there, day after day, waiting for a sign, a glimpse of him, anything that could lead me back to what I had lost. The thought of confronting him again, of reclaiming what was mine, was the only thing that kept me anchored.

As the days passed, my resolve wavered. The hope that had once burned bright within me was now a flickering flame, struggling to stay alight. "I'll just wait on this bench outside his place forever if I have to," I muttered to myself, a desperate vow to a seemingly uncaring universe.

But as I sat there, lost in my despair, a realization began to dawn on me. Perhaps being a witch wasn't all I was. Maybe, just maybe, there was more to me than the magic I had wielded. The thought was both terrifying and liberating. For so long, I had defined myself by my powers, but now, faced with their absence, I was forced to confront the possibility of a different kind of strength – one that came from within, not from spells or enchantments.

As the sun began to set, casting long shadows across the park, I found myself at a crossroads. The future lay before me, uncertain and uncharted. "What can I do?" I asked aloud, the question a whisper in the gathering dusk. It was a cliffhanger, the next page of my story yet to be written. And in that moment of doubt and possibility, I realized that the answer lay not in what I had lost, but in what I had yet to discover about myself.

Chapter 24 - The Spellbound House

Braids:

The days at the park bench blurred into one long, melancholic vigil. The trees around me began to shed their leaves, a silent testament to the passage of time and the changes it brought. I barely noticed the world around me, lost in my own thoughts, until Leon's unexpected visit jolted me back to reality.

He approached me with a cautious determination, his footsteps crunching on the fallen leaves. I looked up, surprised and somewhat annoyed by his presence. "Go away,

Leon," I said sharply, my voice laced with a mix of sadness and irritation. "I don't need your pity."

But Leon didn't leave. He sat down beside me, maintaining a respectful distance, his expression one of genuine concern. "I can help you," he offered softly.

I scoffed, turning my head away. "No, leave me alone," I replied, the words heavy with defeat. I didn't want his help, or anyone's. I wanted to wallow in my misery, to nurse the wounds that Damian had inflicted.

Leon persisted, his voice calm and steady. "What choice do you have? I can take you to the family home. Maybe there's something there that can help you... something that can give you answers."

His words hung in the air between us, a lifeline thrown in the midst of my despair. I knew I had little choice. My options were limited, and my own attempts to reclaim what I had lost had led me nowhere.

With a heavy heart, I nodded, agreeing to his plan begrudgingly. "Fine," I muttered, my voice barely above a whisper. "But don't expect me to be grateful."

Leon helped me to my feet, his gesture kind but unnecessary. I was still strong, still capable, even without my magic. We walked out of the park together, the setting sun casting long shadows on our path.

As we made our way to the family home, a myriad of emotions churned within me – hope, skepticism, fear, and a faint glimmer of curiosity. What would we find there? Could it really help me, or was this just another dead end?

But deep down, I knew this was more than just a search for answers. It was a journey towards understanding – understanding what had happened, understanding Damian's motives, and perhaps, understanding myself. The path ahead was uncertain, but for the first time in days, I felt a flicker of something that had been missing – a sense of purpose, however faint.

The car ride to the family home was a silent journey, each of us lost in our own thoughts. Leon drove with a concentration that bordered on meticulous, his hands steady on the wheel. The landscape outside blurred into a mix of greens and browns, the countryside passing by in a quiet lull.

Leon occasionally attempted to lighten the mood, a quip here, a small joke there, but I wasn't in the mood for banter. My responses were curt, my mood somber. The loss of my powers and the betrayal I had experienced left little room for levity.

After a stretch of silence, I finally broke the quiet. "Why are you even helping me?" I asked, my voice tinged with a mix of suspicion and genuine curiosity.

Leon glanced at me briefly before returning his eyes to the road. "You haven't done anything wrong," he said simply. His voice carried a sincerity that I hadn't expected, making me reconsider my initial impression of him.

His answer left me pensive, the walls I had built around myself starting to crack. Here was Leon, Damian's brother, offering me help – a gesture that seemed to stem from a place of understanding and compassion. It was a stark contrast to Damian's actions, a reminder that not everyone in this tangled mess of a situation was against me.

The rest of the ride was filled with a contemplative silence. Leon's words had struck a chord, making me reflect on the events that had led me to this point. The betrayal, the loss, the anger – they were all still there, but now there was also a faint glimmer of hope, a possibility that maybe, just maybe, I wasn't as alone in this as I had thought.

As we neared our destination, the family home loomed into view – a structure that held secrets and perhaps, answers to the questions that had plagued me. The journey ahead was uncertain, but with Leon's unexpected allyship, I felt a renewed sense of determination to uncover the truth, to find a way to regain what I had lost, and to confront the challenges that lay ahead.

The moment we arrived at the house, I felt a surge of adrenaline course through me. Leon pointed out the destination, but I was already leaping from the carriage, my skirts billowing around me in a flurry of dark fabric. I heard

Leon scrambling after me, his voice calling out, "I have the key!"

But there was no need for keys. The door was surprisingly open. With a swift motion, I grabbed the handle, lifted my skirts, and delivered a forceful kick to the door. It swung open with a loud creak, revealing the sun-strewn parlor beyond.

Inside, the house was eerily quiet, the only sign of life being the elegant furniture that adorned the room. Velvet pillows rested on couches, and coffee tables bore intricate engravings. Books lay scattered about, suggesting recent activity. A cup of tea, its vapor still rising, sat abandoned among the tomes.

Leon caught up to me, his footsteps heavy and his scent of gentleman's perfume permeating the air around us. I turned swiftly, pressing a finger to my lips to signal silence. To my surprise, he gently took my hand and lowered it, his touch unexpectedly soft.

"I'll handle this. I'm his brother," he whispered, a determined look in his eyes.

"He's a dangerous maniac," I growled under my breath, frustration seething within me. "And he's got my candelabra, my spellbook, access to my spells…"

"He's not expecting any trouble from me," Leon replied calmly.

Despite my suspicions, I knew he was right. Reluctantly, I allowed him to take the lead. Leon stepped forward, moving towards the adjacent room, visible through an open archway. "Damian," he called out, his voice echoing in the stillness. "I'm here. It's Leon. Are you home? What are you up to?"

I cringed at his calling out but followed, unable to stay still. My entire being pulsed with a mix of dread and anticipation. This house held the key to my life's work, my passion, something more profound than any facade I had ever put up.

As I crept forward, my gaze was suddenly drawn to a striking sight – a great blue orb, pulsing with electricity, arcs of energy leaping off it. Before I could react, it burst, sending shockwaves through the room. The sound was deafening, a metallic taste filled my mouth, and a numbing sensation overwhelmed my senses.

"Leon…" His name escaped my lips as I lost sight of him around the corner. I wanted to move, to find him, but suddenly, I was rooted to the spot. Waves of confusion washed over me, a spellbinding force that I had never experienced from the receiving end. For the first time, I was under the influence of a spell, and the realization of its strangeness dawned on me. My mind fought against the enchantment, struggling to maintain a grip on reality, but the spell was potent, overwhelming my senses and pulling me into its grasp.

Chapter 25 - A Confrontation's Edge

Braids:

Ensnared in the throes of a spell, a reality unfamiliar and disconcerting, I grappled with the ethereal chains binding my mind. The idea that I, a practitioner of magic, was now on the receiving end of a spell was both ironic and infuriating. It was a lone, flickering star in the dark sea of confusion that engulfed me, and I clung to it, letting it guide me back to a semblance of clarity.

With a herculean effort of will, I began to move, each step a battle against the fog that clouded my senses. My movements were sluggish, heavy, as if I were wading through a dream. I had never considered the need to defend against my own magic. The thought had seemed absurd – until now.

Rounding the corner, I found Leon standing by a desk, bathed in sunlight, his back to me. And there, in the chair, sat a figure I assumed to be Damian, shrouded in shadows. But as the daze began to lift, the fog in my mind clearing, I realized it was a phantom, an illusion. A smirk touched my lips – a classic trick, one I would have been proud of under different circumstances.

As I scanned the room for the real Damian, he suddenly appeared, springing his ambush. He grasped my arms, binding them behind my back with a clumsiness that spoke of his inexperience with magic. Despite his efforts, I was not detained for long. Channeling the strength of my enchanted boots, I delivered a powerful kick backward, the force of it sending Damian flying back with a yowl of pain.

In the chaos, Leon sprang into action, his movements decisive and quick. He was the brawn to my brains in this unexpected partnership. Trusting him was not a choice but a necessity. He launched into a counterattack, his actions driven by panic and instinct. I followed suit, deflecting Damian's feeble attempts at magic, his shock at our combined assault evident on his face.

With a swift roll and a fluid movement, I pinned Damian down, my feet pressing against him in a spell of submission. Leon, seizing the moment, took a photograph, capturing Damian in this humiliating defeat. It was a picture of funny, yet satisfying blackmail – a reminder of the trust I had placed in Leon and the victory we had achieved together.

In the midst of the chaos, Leon was still caught in the grips of the confusion spell, standing frozen and dazed. With no time to waste, I quickly reached out and shook him by the shoulders, attempting to snap him out of his stupor. But before I could see if my efforts had any effect, Damian was on me again, his anger fueling his actions.

Acting on instinct, I darted towards the side door, escaping into what appeared to be a garden. The rows of neatly planted lettuce and tomatoes, bound in sticks and twine, blurred past me as I tore one string free in my hasty retreat. I sprinted towards a sprawling field beyond, the grassy expanse rolling uphill before me.

My flight was desperate and unthinking, a stark contrast to the calculated and strategic moves I was accustomed to when armed with my spells. Damian was relentless in his pursuit, closing the gap between us as we ascended the slope. His hand clasped my arm, pulling me back with a force that sent me crashing against his chest.

For the first time, I found myself face to face with Damian, his features twisted in hate and rage. His brown eyes burned with a fire that was both terrifying and revealing. This close encounter was a far cry from the invisible presence I had maintained during his concert night. The intensity in his gaze spoke volumes of the animosity and tumultuous emotions swirling within him.

I stood there, caught in his grasp, feeling the raw, unbridled fury emanating from him. It was a moment of realization – the man who had once been just a distant part of my magical conflicts was now a tangible, wrathful presence. The hate in his eyes was a reflection of the bitter struggle we were entangled in, a struggle that had transcended mere magical rivalry and delved into something far more personal and profound.

The close proximity to Damian, his furious gaze boring into mine, sent a shiver through me. The raw intensity of his emotions felt eerily familiar, almost like a reflection of my own inner turmoil on a typical day. In that brief, charged moment, a thought flickered through my mind – could the spells, the power and control they grant, be shaping us in ways we never fully realized? I had always seen my magic as an enhancement to my life, but could it also be amplifying my own bitterness?

These thoughts, however, were fleeting. This was not the time for introspection. Damian's shout snapped me back to the present. "It's not yours! You cannot have it! You're a scoundrel. A thief."

His accusation struck me, a mix of shock and indignation washing over me. "It was rightfully found!" I retorted, defending my claim to the candelabra.

"It was always mine, my family, my legacy, to have it!" he countered, his voice laced with possessiveness.

"It was your own mother, who disagreed with it and brought it to me. Take it up with her!" I shot back, trying to pierce through his sense of entitlement.

"But you! You hid the truth from me the moment I entered your shop!" Damian's accusation was like a slap, a reminder of the tangled web of deception and half-truths that had brought us here.

"It's been mine my whole life! And it's everything to me!" My voice rose in a mix of desperation and determination.

"You've had it long enough. It's my time!" he declared, as if that settled everything.

The argument felt childish, two people fighting over what seemed, in that heated moment, like a mere object. Yet, it was so much more than that – it was about legacy, identity, and the paths our lives had taken. It struck me then, the absurdity that we had never considered the possibility of collaboration or sharing. Like children, the concept of working together had eluded us completely.

The notion of partnership taunted me, a bitter reminder of a missed opportunity. There had been a moment, after witnessing the soulful beauty of Damian's music, when I had felt a glimmer of hope. I had thought someone capable of creating such art could understand me, could pull me back from the brink and into the world again. But Damian's possessiveness, his narrow-mindedness, shattered that hope.

He had never considered that I could teach him, that we could share the legacy of the candelabra. His focus was solely on claiming it as his own, a stance that now twisted my stomach with frustration and regret.

As I stood there, locked in this bitter standoff with Damian, a glimpse of a wild hare on the hill caught my attention. It emerged from the forest underbrush, a rare sight in such open space. The sight of the animal sparked a thought in my mind – if only I could find some way to use it. Even without my spellbook, there might be a chance to conjure something, anything, that could turn the tide in my favor.

My eyes darted to Damian's belt. He must have known to carry some powders or components for on-the-go spells, a trick I was all too familiar with. If I could just locate and reach them, I might be able to cast a spell, even in my current state of powerlessness.

I noticed that Damian's left hand, the one gripping mine, was engulfed in unburnt, rippling green fire. It drew my attention, a flicker of hope amidst the desperation. I didn't fully understand how this magic worked, especially when it came to manipulating others' spells, but it was a chance I had to take.

With the twine still in my hands from the garden, I made a quick decision. I flicked the twine towards the green fire of his hand. In an instant, the twine transformed, growing and whipping alive into the form of a snake. It struck, biting him on the upper arm. Damian gasped, recoiling in shock and pain, giving me the brief moment I needed.

I quickly inspected his belt and saw a pouch, undoubtedly containing some kind of power. Without hesitation, I snatched it and flung its contents – some into his eyes, some into the green flaming hand.

Damian cried out in agony, his hands going to his eyes as they visibly shrank on his face. The spell had worked, albeit in a way I hadn't anticipated. For a moment, he was disoriented, blinded by whatever power I had unleashed upon him.

It was a small victory, but it gave me a critical advantage. The tide was turning, and for the first time since this confrontation began, I felt a glimmer of control returning to me. Damian was momentarily vulnerable, and I had to act quickly. This was my chance to reclaim what he had taken, to turn the tables in this relentless struggle between us.

Chapter 26 - Awakening of Purpose

Braids:

The battle escalated rapidly, each of us drawing upon our reserves of skill and desperation. Damian, armed with spells from the book he had taken from me, unleashed them with a novice's fervor but lacked the finesse and understanding that came with a lifetime of practice. I, on the other hand, relied on instinct and the deep well of knowledge I had accumulated over the years. Despite being at a disadvantage without my candelabra and spellbook, I found ways to counter his attacks, turning his inexperience against him.

As we fought, Leon, having recovered from his initial shock, ran into the field, shouting warnings and trying to assist. He was brave, perhaps recklessly so, as he placed himself in the heart of the magical maelstrom. Damian, caught up in his rage and focus on me, lashed out, and Leon was knocked down, sustaining injuries in his effort to help.

The fight was intense and chaotic, spells flying with wild abandon. I could see Leon struggling to his feet, his movements labored but determined. There was a moment of clarity amidst the chaos when Leon, understanding the gravity of the situation, made a crucial decision. With a great effort, he hurled the spellbook towards me, his throw guided by a mix of desperation and hope.

Catching the book, I felt a surge of power and familiarity. It was like being reunited with a part of myself that I had thought lost forever. I flipped through the pages, quickly finding the spells I needed. With the book back in my possession, my confidence surged. I was no longer a witch without her tools; I was Braids, and I was in my element.

Damian, realizing that the tide had turned, redoubled his efforts, hurling spell after spell in a frenzied attempt to overpower me. But with each attack, I countered, my actions guided by a lifetime of knowledge and experience. The battle reached a crescendo, spells colliding with a fury that shook the very air around us.

In the end, it was my experience and deep connection to my magic that gave me the upper hand. I struck with a spell that Damian couldn't counter, a culmination of all my years of practice and understanding. He faltered, overwhelmed by the intensity of my magic, and finally collapsed, defeated.

As the dust settled, I rushed to Leon's side. He lay on the ground, injured but alive, his sacrifice nearly costing him his life. I knelt beside him, my heart filled with gratitude and concern. "Leon, you saved me," I said, my voice thick with emotion.

He managed a weak smile, his eyes reflecting both pain and relief. "I couldn't let you fight alone," he murmured.

Leon's bravery and selflessness had been integral to my victory. He had shown a courage and loyalty that went beyond familial bonds, risking everything to help me reclaim what was mine. As I helped him to his feet, supporting his injured form, I knew that this battle had changed us both. We had faced the darkness together, and in doing so, had forged a bond that would not be easily broken.

In the aftermath of the battle, as I lay there defeated, my eyes found Leon, crumpled on the ground, his body battered from the chaos I had unleashed. The sight of him, my younger brother, injured because of my actions, struck a chord deep within me. It was a jarring realization, a moment of clarity amidst the ruins of my blind ambition.

Guilt washed over me in waves, overwhelming and suffocating. The pursuit of the candelabra, the power, the magic – it had all seemed so crucial, so vital to my existence. But now, seeing Leon hurt, possibly dying, because of me, I understood the true cost of my obsession. In my quest for power, I had lost sight of what truly mattered – my family, my brother, the bond we shared.

Desperation crept into my voice as I turned to Braids, who was now kneeling beside Leon, trying to assess his injuries. "Please," I begged, my voice cracking with emotion. "Can you fix this? Can you save him?"

Braids looked at me, her eyes wide with a mixture of shock and uncertainty. "I... I've never done anything like a healing spell before," she stammered, her hands hovering over Leon, unsure of what to do.

The helplessness in her voice was a mirror of my own. "Please, try," I pleaded, the urgency clear in my tone. "For Leon's sake. He's all I have left."

There was a long, tense moment where time seemed to stand still. Braids took a deep breath, her eyes closing as she focused. I watched, holding my own breath, as she tentatively placed her hands over Leon's wounded form. Muttering under her breath, she began an incantation, her words unsure but filled with a desperate hope.

The air around us hummed with a faint energy, a subtle glow emanating from Braids' hands as she attempted the spell. It was clear she was venturing into uncharted territory, driven by the need to save my brother, to undo the harm I had caused.

As the minutes passed, Leon's breathing steadied, his face relaxing as the pain seemed to ebb away. Braids continued her spell, her concentration unwavering. Slowly, miraculously, Leon's injuries began to heal, the worst of the wounds closing, leaving behind only faint scars.

When Braids finally opened her eyes, there was a look of astonishment on her face, a mixture of relief and disbelief at what she had achieved. Leon stirred, his eyes fluttering open, meeting mine with a weak but recognizable spark of life.

I was overwhelmed with gratitude and relief, but also a profound sense of humility. In my blind pursuit of power, I had nearly destroyed the one person who meant the most to me. This realization marked a turning point, a moment of emotional reckoning. I understood then that some pursuits come at too high a cost, and that true strength lies in knowing what to cherish and protect. My brother's life was more precious than any magic, and from that moment on, I vowed to remember the lesson I had learned so painfully.

As I stood there, the weight of Damian's plea heavy on my shoulders, I knew what I had to do, despite my doubts and fears. Leon's life hung in the balance, and if there was even the slightest chance I could save him, I had to take it. With a deep breath, I steeled myself for the task ahead.

Damian, recognizing the gravity of the situation, reluctantly handed me back the candelabra. Its familiar weight in my hands was a comfort, a reminder of the power I once wielded with ease. Yet, the task at hand was unlike anything I had attempted before. Healing spells were not in my repertoire; my magic had always been about control, manipulation, not restoration.

With Leon lying motionless before me, I focused on the candelabra, drawing upon its energy. I began to chant, my words tentative at first, growing in confidence as I found the rhythm of the spell. The air around us seemed to vibrate with a quiet intensity, the power of the candelabra merging with my will.

But the spell didn't take. Leon's condition remained unchanged, his breaths shallow and labored. Panic began to set in, a cold fear that I might not be able to save him. I tried again, altering the incantation, modifying the energy flow, but the result was the same. Desperation clawed at my heart, each failed attempt amplifying my dread.

I could feel Damian's anxious gaze on me, his hope fading with each passing second. But I couldn't give up. Not now. Not when Leon's life was at stake.

Gathering all my focus, I poured every ounce of my being into the candelabra, channeling my magic with a fervor I had never known before. The spell's words flowed from me, not just as incantations, but as pleas, as cries from the depths of my soul.

Then, finally, something shifted. The energy around us sparked, a warm glow emanating from the candelabra. Leon's body responded, a deep, ragged breath filling his lungs. His chest rose and fell more steadily, the color returning to his cheeks. The spell was working.

The sight of Leon's gradual recovery was nothing short of miraculous, a tangible testament to the untapped potential of my magic. As I stood there, the candelabra still warm in my hands, I was enveloped in a profound sense of awe. My heart, which had been pounding with anxiety and fear, began to settle into a rhythm of quiet wonder.

I had always viewed my magic through a narrow lens, seeing it as a means to bend and shape the world to my will. It had been a tool for control, a way to exert my influence over the elements and forces around me. But now, as I watched the life returning to Leon's body, his breathing growing deeper and more steady, I realized that my magic held capabilities far beyond what I had ever imagined.

The revelation was startling. The power I wielded, which I had often used to create and manipulate, could also heal and rejuvenate. It was a humbling and exhilarating discovery. The energy that flowed through me, once used to command and conquer, now served to mend and revive. It was as if I had uncovered a hidden dimension of my abilities, a facet of my magic that was nurturing and life-giving.

This newfound understanding of my magic's potential filled me with a sense of responsibility and purpose. I was no longer just a witch with formidable powers; I was a guardian of a sacred gift, one that could bring healing and hope. The realization imbued me with a newfound respect for the magic

I had been entrusted with. It was a force that deserved to be wielded with care and wisdom, a power that could create as much as it could destroy.

As Leon's eyes met mine, a silent acknowledgment passed between us. In his gaze, I saw gratitude and a trace of awe mirroring my own. In that moment, I felt a shift within me, a deepening of my connection to the mystical forces I had always embraced but never fully understood. My journey as a witch had taken a new turn, one that promised exploration and discovery of the deeper, more benevolent aspects of my craft.

The relief that flooded through me was palpable, a weight lifting from my shoulders. Leon's eyes fluttered open, meeting mine with a dazed but grateful look. Damian stepped forward, his expression a mix of gratitude and newfound respect.

In that moment, I understood that my magic was more than just a tool or a weapon. It was a gift, one that could bring as much good into the world as it could chaos. And as I stood there, with the candelabra in my hands, I felt a shift within me, a new sense of purpose and possibility for the magic I wielded.

Chapter 27 - Ethereal Bonds

Braids:

With my powers restored and Leon by my side, I found myself on a path I hadn't foreseen. The events that unfolded had changed me, softened edges I had long thought immutable. Standing there, with Leon looking at me with an expression of pure, unguarded affection, I realized that his love was something rare and genuine. It was a love that saw beyond the surface, beyond the grumpiness and darkness that I often wore like armor. Leon had seen me at my lowest, in moments of desperation and vulnerability, and yet, he stood beside me, unwavering in his support.

Feeling a warmth spreading through me, a sensation I wasn't entirely familiar with, I leaned forward and gave Leon a gentle peck on the cheek. It was a small gesture, but it held a universe of meaning. It was an acknowledgment of the bond that had formed between us, a bond forged in the fires of conflict and solidified in mutual respect and understanding.

Some time later, we found ourselves strolling together in the park, the same place where I had spent countless hours in despair and solitude. The scene was different now; the park was alive with the sounds of laughter and conversation, a stark contrast to the silence and introspection of my previous visits. Leon and I walked side by side, our conversation flowing easily, punctuated with laughter and shared glances.

As we walked, Leon spoke candidly, his words filled with affection. "You know, I love you, even though you're grumpy and dark," he said, a playful twinkle in his eye. "Actually, I love that about you. It's part of what makes you, you."

His words struck a chord within me. It was an acceptance of my whole self, shadows and all. For so long, I had seen my darker traits as barriers to connection, yet here was someone who embraced them as part of my identity. Leon's love wasn't just an acceptance of the parts of me that were easy to love; it was an embrace of all that I was, grumpiness, darkness, strength, and vulnerability alike.

The realization that I could be loved for who I truly was felt like a revelation. It was a healing balm to the parts of me that had felt unworthy or too flawed. As we continued our walk, the future seemed brighter, filled with possibilities and a newfound sense of hope. With Leon by my side, I felt ready to face whatever came next, knowing that I had someone who loved me for me, in all my complexity and contradiction.

The evening had brought with it a sense of resolution, a closing of chapters and opening of new ones. I decided to bring Leon to my favorite haunt, the bar where I had spent countless hours in the company of the Gemool, my ghostly companions. As we settled into the dimly lit ambiance of the bar, I turned to Leon, a mischievous glint in my eye.

"Do you trust me?" I asked, my voice tinged with a playful seriousness.

Leon nodded without hesitation. "Yes, I do."

With a knowing smile, I mixed a special elixir into our alcohol shots, a concoction that would allow us to join my ghostly friends in their ethereal realm. Handing him the drink, I said, "Drink this..."

He took the shot, curiosity evident in his gaze. Within moments, we both became invisible to the eyes of the living, our bodies feeling lighter as we ascended towards the ceiling.

Leon's expression transformed into one of amazement as we floated upward, joining the realm where the Gemool resided.

The look on Leon's face when he first saw the ghosts was priceless – a mixture of astonishment and wonder. The spectral figures of the Gemool, with their blue, shimmering forms, were a sight to behold.

Sitting among them, I introduced Leon. "I brought a guest today. Deal us both in," I said, a warmth in my voice that had been absent for so long.

The Gemool, ever the curious spirits, inquired about my day. With a lightness in my heart, I shared, "Guess what? I've changed!"

Their ghostly laughter filled the air, a sound both eerie and comforting. "Good for you!" they chorused. "It never worked for us, but we're glad you figured out a way!"

In that moment, surrounded by my ghostly friends and with Leon by my side, I felt a profound sense of contentment. The grumpiness that had been my constant companion seemed to lift, replaced by a feeling of peace and happiness.

As we played cards with the Gemool, laughing and talking, I realized how far I had come. The journey had been long and fraught with challenges, but it had led me to this moment of joy and acceptance. Leon's presence, the understanding and love he offered, had opened my heart in ways I hadn't thought possible.

The chapter of my life that had been filled with loneliness and strife was closing, and a new one, full of hope and connection, was beginning. The bar, once a refuge from the world, had become a place of celebration – a celebration of change, of love, and of new beginnings.

And so, the book of my life turned to its next chapter, ending on a beautiful note, a testament to the power of change, the strength of love, and the enduring bond of friendship. In the company of the Gemool and Leon, I found a happiness I had never known, a happiness that promised brighter days ahead.

The End.

Dear Reader, Thank you for reading The Witch's Candelabra! If you enjoyed it, please support the author by reviewing it on Amazon (and/or GoodReads) and letting others know about this book!

With Love and Gratitude,

J.B. Lesel